The Last Word: A Novel

Paul Combs

The Stratford Press
USA

The Last Word: A Novel

Printed in the United States of America

ISBN-13: 978-0692235386
ISBN-10: 0692235388

Published by The Stratford Press

10 9 8 7 6 5 4 3 2 1

First Edition

For my girls

"When you sell a man a book you don't sell him just twelve ounces of paper and ink and glue — you sell him a whole new life. Love and friendship and humor and ships at sea by night — there's all heaven and earth in a book." – Christopher Morley, *Parnassus on Wheels*

1

"An Unexpected Note"

Salvatore Terranova hates to sweat, but not as much as he hates the idea of getting fat like every other man in his family. Which is why, in spite of Trenton's unseasonable heat and Sal's aversion to perspiration, he is at the park for his twice-weekly game of pick-up basketball. The game has just ended in a loss, and he is seated on a bench near an asphalt basketball court drinking from a bottle of water. Paulie sits beside him, once again starting a conversation Sal wants no part of.

"So what are you gonna do?" Paulie finally asks. "It's not like it's gonna get any easier for you."

Sal looks at Paulie, wishing he didn't have to discuss this again. He thinks, not for the first time, that Paulie bears a striking resemblance to a young Pacino, *Dog Day Afternoon*-era. Sal is more DeNiro in *Midnight Run*, in bearing if not totally in appearance.

Paulie is wearing a white undershirt that is two sizes too small and short athletic shorts that went out of style in the early 1980s. *Italians should show more class*, Sal thinks. He prefers baggier shirts and long shorts for the court; no need to make your muscles appear bigger by wearing tight clothes. But then, unlike Paulie, he *has* muscles.

"No idea," Sal replies, toweling sweat from his face. "Maybe I should take a vacation, lay low for a while. But how can I leave all this?"

He gestures around at a neighborhood that has clearly seen better days. It's not exactly a ghetto, but its glory days are long past. Nearly half of the storefronts along Union Avenue are vacant; some are boarded up, while others still bear the names of their former occupants. The shops that cling to life see fewer and fewer customers. The place would look great in a Scorsese film, but not in a Chamber of Commerce ad.

"Sure," Paulie says sarcastically. "Paradise Found, that's this place."

"One lousy job," Sal says, shaking his head. "I've been doing this since I was fourteen, hundreds of times probably, and this one gets all the attention. It wasn't even that big a score."

"The cops don't seem to agree."

"Tell me about it. I can't take a leak without the staties or the Feds or some overeager flatfoot there to hold my cock for me."

"There's that other thing, too," Paulie says, then quickly looks away.

"Other thing?"

"Yeah, with the Family. What is it you keep calling it?"

"A misunderstanding with someone's mother," Sal says with a smile.

"Right," Paulie says, then laughs. "Some misunderstanding."

While they are speaking, an older woman, late 60s at least, approaches from the sidewalk. Her hair is in curlers and she wears a housecoat that may have been blue at some point years ago. Her slippers are newer, with little bunny heads at the toes.

She has a slip of paper in her hand. She stops a few feet from Sal, waiting for permission to come forward. He smiles and beckons her over. It is Mrs. Castellano, his landlady.

"I'm sorry to bother you, Salvatore," she says meekly, "but this just came for you, and it seems important. I haven't seen a telegram since I was twelve years old."

She hands the paper to him then quickly retreats, nodding to Paulie as she steps back. Sal reads the telegram and his face drops.

"You look like somebody died, pal," Paulie says.

"Somebody did."

Sal looks up from the telegram to see that Mrs. Castellano has leveled a .38 Smith and Wesson revolver at his head. This would be more startling if it wasn't such a common occurrence.

"Jeez, Mrs. C, if I'm late on the rent you could just tell me."

"I'm really sorry about this, Sally," she says, her hazel eyes suddenly bright, "but I'm an old woman on a fixed income and—"

"You own six boarding houses," he interrupts. "Hardly a fixed income."

"That's true, dear, but regardless. I know you've got something big stashed from that business up in Ithaca, and—"

"Oh c'mon, Mrs. C. Not you too!"

Sal rises to his feet and Mrs. Castellano takes a step back, the gun still steady on him. She is barely five feet tall and less than one hundred pounds; he is a foot taller and eighty pounds heavier. But she is too far away for him to lunge at her, and she knows it.

"Please stop interrupting me, dear," she scolds him as if he were an unruly child. "As I was saying, I don't want all of it, of course, but I—"

At that moment a basketball slams into the side of Mrs. Castellano's face, knocking the tiny woman off her feet. The gun skitters toward Sal when she hits the pavement, and he quickly picks it up. He looks over to the court, where Manny, a wiry Dominican man in his early 20s, is grinning maniacally at him.

"Thanks, pal," Sal says. "I owe you one."

"Don't mention it," Manny says, still grinning like a madman. "When you finally go down, it's gonna be me who does it, not some old *abuela*."

"That's comforting."

Sal looks back at Paulie, who is leaning down over Mrs. Castellano.

"She okay?" he asks.

"Yeah, she'll be fine. You should probably look for a new apartment, though."

Sal shakes his head and stuffs the gun in his gym bag.

"Now I got senior citizens pulling guns on me."

Paulie simply shrugs and nudges the prone form of Mrs. Castellano with his foot. She stirs slightly and emits a soft moan. "There goes the neighborhood," he says.

The next day, on the other side of the Atlantic in a posh London office building, Camden Templeton-Smoot strides confidently down a thickly carpeted hall to her boss's office. She is dressed professionally as always; none of this "Casual Friday" nonsense for her. The black pumps make her several inches taller than her actual height of five foot six. They are uncomfortable, of course, as walking on pointy sticks is not natural, but they do make her calves look good. Her dark blonde hair is tied up in a bun.

Once inside the spacious corner suite with a breathtaking view of the Millennium Bridge and the London Eye, her boss gestures impatiently for her to sit. She takes a seat opposite him at a massive oak desk and thinks, not for the first time, that her employer looks remarkably like a ferret. The small ferret-man taps a sheaf of papers with his index finger and shakes his head sadly.

"I understand we all make mistakes, Ms. Templeton-Smoot," he says, skipping past the usual inane pleasantries, "but most don't cost the client, and by extension potentially the firm, over half a million pounds."

Camden sits even straighter in her seat, which makes her more than a head taller than her boss, who is normal-sized for a ferret but quite small for a man.

"I moved the funds exactly as the client requested," she replies calmly. "He had the hot tip, he insisted over my protestations, and it's his own bloody fault the Tax Man found what he was doing."

"Yes, yes. I see your point, of course." Her boss nods in apparent agreement. "But it does look bad for us, Camden. We pride ourselves on our ability to creatively, but legally, protect clients' assets from the Crown."

"Are they investigating us?" she asks, alarmed.

"No, nothing like that, thank heavens. But for appearances sake we must make some sort of gesture."

There is a long pause during which they stare at each other. Camden knows the first to speak usually loses, but staring down a ferret is no small task. She finally gives in.

"You're sacking me."

"Quite," replies the ferret-man, relieved he doesn't have to actually say the words himself. "No hard feelings."

An hour later, having cleaned out her desk and received the final paycheck that was already cut and waiting for her, she emerges from the Finsbury Park Underground station, her mood dark. During the long tube ride she read an article in *The Guardian* that cruelly detailed how, after managing only a draw against Portsmouth, Arsenal had slipped to 4 points behind arch-rival Tottenham Hotspur for the final Champions League place and now has virtually no hope of catching Chelsea for the Premier League title. An ardent football fan, she lives and dies according to the fortunes of her beloved Gunners, and this latest setback is almost too much to bear. Arsenal's unbeaten Premier League campaign of 2003-2004 seems as far away as her now-shattered career.

After several blocks she turns down a short lane, stopping at the door of the small flat she shares with her husband, Giles Smoot. She fumbles in her bag for a moment, trying to locate her key, then finds it and unlocks the door. She drops the box containing the few personal items she had at her office on the floor and marches straight to the kitchen for tea, grabbing a worn paperback romance novel from an end table along the way.

Entering the kitchen, she stops short when she finds her husband at the table with his doubles badminton partner, Albert Spencer, drinking tea. At 39, Giles is eight years older than her; Albert is perhaps eight years younger. Both are completely naked, and when they see her they make no move to cover themselves.

"'Morning love," Giles says cheerfully. "You're home a bit early, no?"

She struggles to remain calm. Clearly she is still asleep and this is a horrible, horrible dream, for it simply cannot be happening. *Though this does explain a few things,* she thinks.

"A bit early, yes," she answers. "If you don't mind me asking, just what in the bloody hell are you playing at?"

Giles nods as if this is a very astute question. Albert adds sugar to his tea and acts as if this scene is a completely normal one.

"Actually I've been meaning to have a word with you about our...hmmm...relationship. You've just been working so much."

"Really. And?"

"Bluntly put, I'd have to say it's no longer viable," he says with a firm nod. "Surely you can see my point."

Camden's gray eyes flash with anger and her gaze falls on a knife on the table; Albert quickly slides it out of reach. She turns without answering and heads out of the kitchen. Giles calls after her.

"By the way, a telegram came for you this morning."

"A what?" she asks without turning back to face him.

"A telegram. Quite a surprise to me, I must say. I didn't know those even existed anymore. It's on the hall table."

She walks to the table and picks up a small folded sheet of paper, then reads it. Her expression changes from anger to sadness, and a tear streams down her face. She tucks the note in her pocket and walks to the bedroom.

Two days later, Camden is seated in the waiting area of the law firm of Billings, Radcliff, and Hurst. She speaks into her cell phone in a hushed voice.

"I have no idea who it is, Mum," she says. "The barrister just gave me the time of the meeting and said one other person would be at the reading of the will."

She pauses, listening.

"No, I missed the funeral. I only just got in last night. The flight from LaGuardia to DFW was delayed because of bad weather."

She pauses again.

"I'm fine, Mum, really. I hope the two buggers live happily ever after. And I'm dropping the 'Smoot' from my name, obviously."

A final pause.

"Yes, I'll call you later today and let you know the outcome. With no job and no home, I better have inherited the Crown Jewels."

She puts the phone in her purse and at that moment the bell over the front door chimes. She looks up to see Sal surveying the room. When he sees her, there is a flicker of recognition by both of them. He steps forward.

"Cam?"

"Sal?"

She rises from her chair, but before she can take one step toward him he is across the room, enveloping her in a bear hug.

"Good lord," he says, "you haven't changed a bit in, what, ten years?"

"Longer, I think."

She steps out of the embrace and looks at him.

"You look good. Has life been treating you well?"

"Depends on your definition of 'well'," he says. "Still never convicted, which is nice."

"Right."

Before they can speak further, a short, stout, middle-aged man appears from an adjacent hallway. Unlike many men his age, he has a surprisingly thick mop of dark hair that he brushes out of his eyes before he speaks.

"You're both here," he says. "Splendid. I'm Robert Billings. Please follow me."

He leads them down a hall hung with English hunting prints that would not have been out of place in Camden's old firm. The hall ends at a large office. Billings' desk is clear except for a large manila envelope and a photograph of what must be his children, a boy and a girl, both in their late teens or early twenties. They all take a seat; Camden and Sal wait for him to speak.

"I know this is a difficult time for both of you," he says softly, "so soon after Mr. Templeton's passing."

They both stare at him, then at each other, then back at him.

"Well, yeah, I suppose," Sal says.

"Certainly, but..." Camden replies.

The lawyer smiles and relaxes visibly; he loosens the knot of his tie.

"Maybe I should start over," he says, leaning back in his chair. "How long has it been since either of you saw your late uncle?"

"Years," Camden says. "At least ten."

"Closer to five for me," Sal says after giving it some thought. "I was through here on...well, let's just call it business."

He smiles at Camden triumphantly; he wins. She rolls her eyes and looks away.

"I see," Billings says, rubbing his chin with his thumb and forefinger. "So neither of you were particularly close to him. From what I can ascertain he was not close to many people. In fact, you two are the only ones mentioned in his will."

This surprises them. Their extended family is certainly large enough for there to be multiple heirs to whatever Franklin left upon his passing.

"Only us?" Camden asks. "I'm just a niece he hardly ever saw. We exchanged a few letters over the years, some Christmas cards, but still..."

"And I'm the blackest sheep this family has," Sal says. "I also wrote some, and occasionally bought a few books that he would mail me, but not enough to warrant this. Whatever this is."

"What about the rest of the family?" Camden asks.

"As you surely know, Franklin never married and had no children," Billings replies. "My guess is that he didn't get on well with his siblings."

"That's true," Sal says. "I don't much either these days."

Camden gives him a quizzical look. He shrugs.

"In any case," Billings continues, "you two are his joint heirs. You have each inherited half of his estate."

Camden's eyes brighten, but Sal's expression remains unchanged.

"What exactly makes up his estate?" Camden asks a little too quickly. "If I don't sound too greedy asking?"

This time Sal rolls *his* eyes. He appears disinterested, but listens attentively. Billings laughs and shuffles through the papers.

"Not greedy at all; that's why we're here today. The estate consists of your uncle's bookstore downtown—all of its contents, inventory, fixtures, etc.—the contents of his apartment above the store, and the cash in his bank accounts."

Billings proceeds to read the details of the will, like legal matters and so forth. Soon he comes to the end.

"Finally, your uncle asked that this DVD be shown to the staff of the store. After you watch it first, of course."

When he has finished, Camden looks at Sal, who merely shrugs again. They sign some papers and rise to leave.

"I don't suppose you would be interested in simply buying out my half?" she asks Sal.

"Not especially."

"Selling me your half?"

"Not a chance, and you couldn't afford it anyway."

"Fine. But I know who you are, Salvatore Terranova."

"Really? I'm flattered. And it may surprise you to learn that I know plenty about you, Mrs. Templeton-Smoot."

"Just Templeton, wiseguy."

He opens the door for her and makes an exaggerated bow. "I guess we should go check out our new bookstore."

2

"I Have Never Begun a Business with More Misgiving"

An hour later, Camden and Sal stand just inside the entrance of Franklin Templeton Booksellers, marveling at what they have just gotten themselves into. The building itself is a stand-alone two-story structure on the corner of Houston Street and Goliad Avenue. This sets it apart from the rest of the block; every other building seems to have used the existing wall of its neighbor, forming the one long row common in older downtown areas across the country. To the left is a small green space with two large oak trees and a bench close to the sidewalk; to the right a narrow alley separates it from the rest of the buildings on Houston.

It is red brick in a Victorian design, though clearly newer than that, probably built in the 1920s. This also makes it unlike its neighbors, which are more 1940s or 50s vintage. The façade possesses an aura of order and stability. The inside is another matter entirely, and Sal and Camden have very different reactions to this.

The place has an old-world charm, Sal thinks. There is a wonderful smell of old leather and paper, like in a 19th century London shop. Camden might agree, if she could see past the layers of dust, disorganized displays, overstuffed shelves, and no customers. A few employees mill about, trying to look busy. Camden and Sal look at each other, and Sal grins broadly. She smacks him in the back of the head.

"What the heck?" he says, rubbing his head and glaring at her.

"Seriously?" she replies. "You seriously want to make a go of *this* place?"

She doesn't wait for an answer. Instead, she locks the front door and flips the sign to CLOSED. A young woman at the front counter stares at her in alarm, thinking this must be a robbery. Sal sees the concern on her face and tries to appear reassuring.

"What's going on here?" asks an older man who strides purposefully toward them. He wears a tasteful gray suit and has a shock of white hair clearly losing its battle with a receding hairline

"Who are you?" Camden asks him.

"Jacob Weinberg," he says. "I run this store."

The girl at the counter rolls her eyes. Sal steps forward; he towers over the old man, but the man does not back up.

"Maybe you did," Sal says. "We do now."

"What do you mean?" he asks.

"We're Franklin Templeton's niece and nephew," Sal tells him, "so like I said, we run the place now. I don't suppose you have a TV with a DVD player in this place?"

"This is a bookshop," Jacob replies indignantly. "Why would we need a television?"

"We don't have a computer either, or a credit card machine," the girl at the counter says, trying to be helpful. "In fact, we still make a carbon of the card on the slide thingy. It's all very retro, in an unintentional way."

Camden stares daggers at Sal, but she's too far away to slap him this time.

"No sweat. I'll be right back," Sal says, and walks out the door.

The employees eye Camden nervously as Sal leaves. She simply looks around the shop again, shaking her head.

In the back room of the store, Cam, Sal, Jacob, and the rest of the staff are huddled around a small television set. Sal is attaching cables from a DVD player to the television, and having some difficulty. Camden stands beside him, pointing.

"The red cable goes there," she says.

"I've got this, okay?" Sal answers.

"Just because you've high-jacked truckloads of electronics doesn't mean you know how to work them."

"At least I didn't need a butler to work the remote for me."

"I did not have a butler!" Camden screams at him, causing everyone else in the room to move back a few steps.

"Whatever, your highness. It's ready." He turns to the assembled group. "This is part of my uncle's last testament," he says. "Since it impacts everyone here, we thought it best that you hear it directly from him."

The screen shows an image of an older man in a conservative suit. His hair is dark, either from good genes or hair coloring, and he has piercing blue eyes. Franklin Templeton looks younger than his 75 years. He is seated at a desk, staring directly into the camera.

"If you're watching this, I am obviously dead," he says evenly. "I hate this video crap, but who the hell can understand that stuff they put in wills except the bloodsucking lawyers? Anyway, I hope I at least went out with a bang."

There is murmuring in the room, and Sal stops the video.

"Let's get it out of the way so everyone can pay attention," he says. "We all know my uncle died in the course of a strenuous, shall we say, *therapy session* with his nurse."

"She was 25," whispers Julia Hall, the young woman who was at the counter.

"And he was 75," says Jacob Weinberg, not whispering.

"So he went out with a bang," Sal replies. "Just like he wanted." He starts the video again.

"My bookstore," Templeton says, "has been my life for more than 50 years. It's the only thing of any value I own, and since I hate most of the Cretans who share my bloodline, I'm leaving it to you, Camden and Sal. You get it all: the store, the books, the apartment upstairs, the staff. I don't technically own them, but I should."

Sal laughs at this; no one else does.

"You may balk at the idea of running a bookstore, but hear me out. Camden, we don't talk much, but I do know that those bean counters you work for are weasels."

"Ferrets," Camden says under her breath.

"If you spend your life there it will kill your soul. Salvatore…well, son, you need a career with a longer life expectancy before you actually do get killed. Since the two of you are the only members of my family who aren't completely worthless, I'm offering you a new start."

Camden looks at Sal, who nods.

"I know this will require a major change for both of you, but I guarantee in a year's time you'll wonder how you were ever happy doing anything else. That's it. Now go sell some damn books."

Sal turns off the television and stands next to Camden at the front of the room. "I know this is both sudden and unexpected," she says. "And you don't know me or my cousin. But I hope you will all stay on and help us fulfill my late uncle's wishes. The store will remain closed today to give us a chance to meet with each of you and get an idea where things stand."

The employees stare blankly at her, and Sal gives her a thumbs-up.

"So, who wants to go first?" she asks.

Julia steps forward immediately, and the others drift out of the room. She is twenty-five years old, with deep brown eyes and light brown hair tied back in a low ponytail. She wears what used to be called librarian glasses, and Sal immediately thinks that while she is attractive now, without the glasses and the hair loose she is most likely a stunner. *Put it out of your mind,* he thinks quickly, *you're the boss now.* The three of them take a seat at a small table.

"Let's see…I'm Julia Hall," the girl says, a little hesitantly. "I guess I told you that earlier." She looks down at her hands, which are folded in her lap.

"No need to be nervous," Camden assures her. Julia glances at Sal, then nods.

"Your uncle referred to me as 'the stable one' since I've been here over two years when most of the staff turns over every few months."

"Every few months?" Camden replies. "Why so often?"

"Well, it doesn't pay a lot," Julia says. "People work in bookstores because they love books, not to get rich. Some people realize they'd rather make more money. That's part of it."

"And the other part?" Sal asks.

Julia hesitates before answering.

"Not to speak ill of the dead, because he was wonderful to me" she says, "but your uncle was not always an easy man to work for. And Jacob Weinberg, as you've already seen, can be an ass."

They both nod.

"But you apparently like it here," Camden says, "if you've stayed for two years."

"Definitely," she says. "I took the job right after college. All I've ever wanted to do is work around books."

"What was your major?" Sal asks.

"English Literature."

"Ah," Camden says, barely hiding her disdain.

"You got a problem with English Literature?" Sal asks. "You're English, for crying out loud."

"No," Camden says. "I just prefer, um, non-fiction." *And trashy romance novels*, she doesn't add.

"You would," he replies.

Julia smiles uncomfortably, not wanting to get in the middle of a squabble between her two new bosses. Sal turns his attention back to her.

"Anyway, since you've been here the longest—"

"Second-longest," she interrupts. "Jacob's been here forever."

"Okay," Sal concedes. "Second-longest. What do you think the place needs most? As far as improvements go, I mean."

"Everything," she replies without hesitation.

"Everything?" Camden asks, surprised by her quick response.

"Yep, everything. I honestly don't know how we've stayed in business. No computerized inventory, no credit card terminal, no focus on merchandising the books...you know, displays and such. And I don't think Franklin was much of a bookkeeper; the deposits he'd send me to the bank with rarely matched the receipts from the day before."

"Wow, that's quite a list," Sal says. "Anything else?"

She nods and continues, clearly over her nervousness.

"A few other things come to mind. He let Jacob fill the store with cool antiquarian books that we'll never sell in a hundred years. We need better lighting and more bestsellers. And a better staffing model wouldn't hurt."

"Staffing model?" Camden asks.

"You see, there are only a few full-time employees. Actually, there are two, not counting you: me and Jacob. Everyone else is part-time."

"That's not so unusual, is it?" Sal asks.

22

"It's actually quite low for a store our size. The thing is, besides Ramon, who works after school and on weekends, I recently counted twenty-seven part-time staff still listed on our payroll. And they basically come in whenever they want."

"Why on Earth would my uncle allow that?" Camden asks.

Julia blushes slightly and does not answer. Camden starts to press for an answer, but Sal stops her.

"That's enough for now, I think. We'll talk more soon, Julia. Thank you."

She nods quickly, relief showing in her expression. Camden looks questioningly at Sal, and he shakes his head slightly. Julia gets up to leave, but stops at the door and looks back.

"Can I ask something without you getting mad?" she asks Sal.

"Of course," he replies. "We're all one big happy, dysfunctional family here."

"You're Sally Fingers, aren't you?"

Camden glances at Sal with an arched eyebrow, and Sal suddenly looks wary.

"Why do you ask?" he says, his eyes narrowing.

"It's just that I was watching a show on Crime TV and it was profiling an unsolved burglary of a fancy house where an un-crackable safe got cracked. They showed a picture of you, younger than you are now, and said you were a prime suspect. I think it was in Buffalo." She says all of this without taking a breath.

"Don't believe everything you see on TV, darlin'," Sal says.

Her shoulders slump. She nods and starts to move through the doorway.

"Julia," he says before she reaches the office door.

She turns back again and looks at him sheepishly.

"It was Ithaca," Sal says with a smile. "And I was in Atlantic City that night. All of my alibis say so."

She nods again, beams at him, then leaves.

"Good lord," Camden says. "I think the girl is smitten with you."

"Smitten," Sal repeats. "That's a good word. And why wouldn't she be?"

Camden rolls her eyes and calls in the next employee. Ramon Sanchez enters and sits down. He is 17 and muscular, with a broad chest and biceps the size of most men's thighs.

"Hi," he says. "I'm Ramon Sanchez."

"Tell us about yourself, Ramon," Camden says after offering him a bottle of water, which he politely declines.

"Well, I'm a high-school junior, and I work after class and weekends shelving books, unloading boxes, cleaning, pretty much everything."

"You like it here?" Sal asks.

"I do," he answers. "It sure beats working as a dishwasher or fast food lackey. I also like it because your uncle has a good section on Latin American history and politics."

"So you're interested in politics?" Sal asks.

"Very much, sir. My Uncle Luis says knowing my heritage and getting involved is the only way I will ever lift my people out of bondage. We're working on a manifesto together, when he has time."

Sal and Camden exchange glances.

"That's....interesting," Camden says.

"Yes, ma'am. My uncle is a very great man."

"Would I have heard him?"

"Oh no," Ramon replies. "He's not famous or anything. His name is Luis Ortiz."

Sal leans forward a little.

"Did your uncle ever live in Virginia Beach?" he asks.

"He did, actually. How did you know?"

"Lucky guess."

Both Ramon and Camden stare at him for a moment, but let it pass without comment.

"Anyway," Camden says, "is there anything you would do to improve things here?"

"Nothing I can think of. Like I said, I like it here. I especially like the Sirens."

"The Sirens?" she asks.

"Yes, ma'am. That was your uncle's name for the group of ladies who work here part-time. He said they were football...I mean soccer moms looking for something to kill the boredom. They're nice to me, and sometimes they'd stay after closing time to help him."

"Like the nurse helped him," Sal says under his breath. "Franklin is becoming my new hero."

"Shush," Camden tells him. She looks back at Ramon. "Thank you, Ramon. We look forward to working with you."

He smiles and leaves.

"That explains Julia's hesitance in explaining all the part-time staff, I guess," Camden says. "Why did he call them the Sirens, I wonder?"

"Easy," Sal answers. "Greek mythology. The song of the Sirens was irresistible, even though it lured the sailors who followed it to their deaths. Don't they teach *The Odyssey* in England?"

She looks at him like she's not sure if he's pulling her leg.

"The Sirens," Sal says, shaking his head. "I think I'm going to like it here."

The final employee to meet with them is Jacob Weinberg; he is clearly not happy about being interviewed by these upstarts.

"So, Jacob, tell us what you do here," Camden says in her most pleasant voice.

"A better question would be what *don't* I do here?" he says without a hint of humor. "But my main job is buying, marketing, and selling the store's inventory of rare and collectible books. Everyone knows that's where the money is, and I've been doing it since before either of you were born."

"I think maybe we got off on the wrong foot earlier," Sal says, trying to sound conciliatory and failing miserably.

"It may have been the wrong foot," Jacob says, cutting him off, "but it was likely indicative of what our relationship will be."

"And what makes you say that?" Camden asks.

"It's clear neither of you knows anything about books, especially your cousin. Frank told me what he does for a living."

Sal starts to speak again, but Camden stops him. "What don't we know, for example?"

"What's the point on *The Sun Also Rises?*" he asks after thinking for a moment.

Camden looks at him like he's speaking a foreign language.

"A point?" she asks. "What is—?"

"The 'stoppped' on page 181, line 26 of the first printing," Sal answers, interrupting her. "Three p's. Seriously, give me a challenge next time."

Both Jacob and Camden look at him in astonishment.

"I wouldn't have thought—" Jacob says.

"That a greaseball thug like me would know that? Your mistake."

"What is a point?" Camden asks.

"Cam," he says, "a 'point' is anything that sets an edition apart, like a misspelled word in a first printing."

"Like three p's in the word 'stopped.'"

"Right," Sal says. "Those are more collectible because there are far fewer of them. Supply and demand, just like anything else."

She nods and turns back to Jacob.

"You seem especially upset that we're here," she says. "Why is that?"

"If you want the truth, I expected Frank would leave the store to me. After all, we've worked together for nearly 30 years. I was closer to him than any of his family."

"So that means you'll be leaving us, then?" Sal asks. His tone is hopeful.

"Well, no," Jacob says, lowering his eyes, his indignation evaporated. "I'd rather stay on, if it's all the same to you."

"Why?" Sal asks.

"Because my wife has told me for the last 10 years that as soon as I retire we're moving to Arizona to live with her sisters. That would be worse than working for you. No offense."

"Fair enough," Camden says, trying not to laugh at the old man.

"So we're going to have to come to some sort of truce, I suppose," Sal says. "I'm sure—"

He is cut off by a loud commotion at the front of the store. The three of them rush from the back to find two people standing by the front counter. One clearly does not belong there.

3

"A New Sheriff in Town"

"I opened the door to let Kate in," Julia explains. "She brought us cupcakes. *He* barged in behind her."

A lanky man in his mid-40s extends his hand to Sal, who ignores it. Camden is immediately reminded of a taller version of her ferret ex-boss.

"Randal Crain," he says. "I own Crain Rare Books on 5th Street. Thought I'd come by and take one last look before you close up the place." He does not even acknowledge Camden.

"What makes you think we're closing, Randy?" Sal asks. As he expected, Randal reacts to the name 'Randy' as if he smelled something unpleasant.

"I just assumed that with old Templeton gone the shop would close. I might even make you an offer myself; I could put my lower-end books down here." He looks around as if already organizing his future shelf space.

"I'll tell you where you can put your books, Crain," Jacob spits out.

"Shouldn't you be back at the nursing home, old man?"

Camden has not spoken, but she senses that a line has just been crossed. She glances at Sal, but he is already moving. Before she can speak, Sal has moved into Crain's personal space.

"If you speak to my late uncle's friend disrespectfully again, Randy," he says in a menacingly level tone, "you'll wish you hadn't."

Crain takes a step back. "Are you threatening me? Do you have any idea who I am?"

"I'm not threatening you, Randy," Sal answers. "I'm warning you. Once. And I've known people like you my whole life."

He keeps his eyes on Randal, and for a moment there is complete silence in the shop. Then Sal lets out a heavy sigh.

"Julia," he says over his shoulder, "be a peach and call 9-1-1."

"What do I tell them?" she asks. Her voice is shaky but excited.

"Tell them I just shot an intruder."

Randal smiles condescendingly until Sal pulls a Glock 9mm from under his jacket, then he lets out a yelp and turns to run. He crashes through the front door, falls to the sidewalk, leaps up and runs down the street. Sal turns and winks at Julia, who blushes slightly.

The whole time this has been going on, an attractive woman in a brightly colored apron has been standing there, frozen in place by the scene. She is in her late 40s and holds a tray of tasty-looking cupcakes. Ramon hurries up to her and takes the tray.

"Thank you, Ms. Jenkins," he says, setting the tray on the counter. "Mr. Sal, Ms. Camden…this is Ms. Kate Jenkins. She owns the bakery two doors down. Ms. Jenkins, these are our new owners."

She shakes hands with Camden and nods admiringly at Sal, who has walked to the counter and grabbed a cupcake while tucking the pistol back in his belt.

"First day and it's already more exciting than it's been around here in years," Kate says.

"Just a normal day for me," Sal replies, taking a bite out of the cupcake. "Mmmm, piña colada. Very good."

Sal and Ramon stand outside a bar downtown where the staff, plus Kate, is continuing to get to know each other. At the door to the Dream Emporium, Sal realizes they may have a hard time getting Ramon in, given that he's only 17. He pulls Ramon aside.

"I didn't think about your age when Kate suggested this place," he says. "Maybe we should go somewhere else."

"Not to worry, sir," Ramon replies. He pulls out his wallet and produces multiple identification cards, from a drivers' license to a social security card to an expired TCU student ID. They all show his age as 23. "Uncle Luis takes care of me," he says with a smile. Sal gives him a knowing look, nods, and they enter the bar.

The Dream Emporium is housed in a two-story art deco building on the corner of Houston and 3rd Street, just down the block from the bookstore. It takes up nearly half the block, and with good reason: this is no neighborhood pub. The first floor boasts a four-star restaurant, the second a dance club that converts into a live music venue, and the rooftop patio graces patrons with an unobstructed view of the moon reflecting off the Trinity River to the north and the crowds of revelers filling Sundance Plaza to the east. Sal and Ramon climb the stairs to the roof.

Everyone is seated at a large table, and a waitress is taking drink orders. Ramon orders a coke and says he is the designated driver; Sal gives him a wink. Before the waitress leaves, Sal whispers something in her ear. Camden sees this, and rolls her eyes.

"I love the view of the city from here at night," Julia says in an attempt to break the ice.

"Not as nice as London," Camden says. "Obviously."

"Better than Trenton," Sal counters.

"I wish I was home reading," Jacob says.

"Come the revolution..." Ramon mumbles.

"I just knew this was the best place for a get-together," Kate gushes.

An uncomfortable silence ensues until the waitress returns. She places the drinks on the table, winks at Sal, then leaves. Sal raises his beer mug.

"To new friends and new opportunities," he says.

There is mumbled agreement, then everyone drinks. Suddenly Camden has a strange look on her face, and she turns and spits out her beer, narrowly missing Sal, who is barely containing his laughter.

"My beer is hot!" she screams. "Bloody hell. Why are you smiling?"

"I thought you Brits always drank beer warm," he says innocently. "I asked the waitress to heat it up for you."

"We don't always drink it warm, you twit. And we never drink Mexican beer warm."

"My mistake," he says. "So, let's get to know each other... I'll start." He takes another drink and looks around the table. "I'm what you'd call the black sheep of the Templeton line, which is only slightly worse than being the English sheep."

Camden slaps him in the back of the head; he ignores her.

"My mom was a Templeton who married into an Italian family in New Jersey."

"Not just any Family," Camden mutters.

"Ignore her," he says. "Camden is jealous of my rich cultural heritage, which gave you the Caesars, the Renaissance, and Frank Sinatra. Hers gave you kidney pie, warm beer, and Margaret Thatcher. Anyway, I moved down here because I needed a change, and my uncle has given me that opportunity, God rest his soul."

"Not running from something?" Jacob asks. "I saw that Crime TV episode about you."

"Does everyone in this town watch that damn show?" he replies. "I was in Hartford that night."

"Atlantic City," Julia corrects him.

"Right, Atlantic City." He smiles at her, and she blushes. "My move here was actually necessitated by a misunderstanding with someone's mother."

"Someone's mother?" Ramon repeats.

"Don't ask," Sal replies. "Regardless, I know a lot about books and not a lot about selling them, but my lack of formal business skill is offset by my cousin here, who knows all kinds of business stuff but nothing about books."

She starts to hit him again, but he blocks it.

"You're gonna need to stop doing that," he says. "Tell them about you."

Camden looks at the group, suddenly nervous. She clears her throat, starts to take a drink, but stops when she realizes it's still the warm beer.

"Well, as you can tell I came here from the UK," she says, speaking very quickly at first. "My dad was a Templeton, and my mum was from London. I'm trained as an accountant, but a bad job and a worse husband made coming to the States an attractive option."

"So we're all escaping something," Sal says.

"Yes," Camden answers. "But Scotland Yard isn't looking for *me*."

"What a coincidence," Sal says. "They're not looking for me either. Yet."

Jacob stands and throws some money on the table. He has clearly had enough of this banter and is about to leave.

"Problem, Jacob?" Sal asks.

"No problem, young man. No problem at all, unless you consider that the business I've devoted my life to is about to become a cross between *Fawlty Towers* and *The Sopranos*."

"I think it will be fun," Julia says. "Having someone with a new perspective on things will liven up the store."

Jacob stops, sits back down, and leans toward her.

"Antiquarian bookstores aren't supposed to be lively, Julia" he says gravely. "They're serious, studious, almost Dickensian places."

"Then only one bowl of gruel a day for you," Sal says in a questionable British accent.

"No matter how many times you say, 'Please, sir, can I 'ave some more?'" Camden adds, her accent much better than Sal's.

The cousins look at each other and smile.

"It will be the best of times," Julia says.

"And the worst of times," Ramon interjects.

Jacob tries to maintain a sour look, but he can't hold it. He finally raises his wine glass.

"Well, if this is how it has to be," he says, "then God bless us, every one."

At that moment a stunning woman in her late-30s walks up behind Sal, slips a piece of paper under his glass and mouths "call me" in his ear, then walks away.

"This sure is a friendly town," Sal says as he unfolds the paper.

"Surely you're not going to call that brazen strumpet?" Cam says indignantly.

"He doesn't have to," Ramon says. "He'll see her at the store tomorrow. She's one of the Sirens."

"Like I said before," Sal says with a smile, "I think I'm going to like it here."

Later that night, Sal is climbing the stairs at the back of the bookshop with Camden right behind him. The stairs lead to Uncle Franklin's apartment.

"It's not morbid," he says. "It's ours now. We need to check it out."

Cam grunts in response, not prepared to start poking around in her uncle's apartment so soon after his death. When they reach the door at the top of the stairs, they discover it is locked.

"Did the lawyer give you a key?" he asks her.

"No," she replies. "Maybe he forgot about the key. Or maybe it's downstairs. I'll go look."

"No need," he says, pulling an odd-looking tool from his pocket. Before she can ask what he's doing the door is open and Sal is inside.

In some ways the apartment is what you would expect from a 75-year-old bookselling bachelor. The furniture seems to have been rescued from various yard sales 20 years earlier, there is dust everywhere, and few pictures hang on the walls. It is where Franklin ate and slept, but his life was apparently downstairs in the bookshop.

A few things do stand out, though. There is a king-sized bed that dominates the bedroom, with handcuffs on each post of the headboard. An expensive video camera on a tripod stands at the foot of the bed. A large number of videocassettes line a shelf on one wall.

"Good Lord!" Camden exclaims. "I don't even want to think about what's on those tapes."

"I should probably check them out," Sal says with a smile. "Just to be thorough."

She tries to slap him, but he dodges the blow. They walk back through the living room and into the kitchen. The large pantry is completely empty; Franklin obviously was not much for cooking.

"Wow," Sal says. "Think about how many crumpets you could fit in there."

"Shut your face," Cam replies. She looks around, sizing up the apartment. "I suppose it might work. I do need a place after all."

"Not so fast there, Hermione," Sal replies. "Who says you get the place? It makes more sense for the single man to live here, just like Uncle Frank did."

"Does not. It makes more sense for a newly-single woman in a strange country who has nowhere else to go to live here."

"Going for the sympathy angle right off the bat, huh?"

"Is it working?" she asks.

"No."

"Be practical, Sal. Everything I said is true, plus I don't own a car; you do. I can live right where I work and not need one."

"What if I gave you my car? But I have to warn you: the steering wheel is on the wrong side."

"Nice try, Guido. Why do you want it so bad, anyway?"

"Did you not see that bed?" he replies.

"Ick. Uncle Frank died there."

"He did a lot more than that." Sal hesitates for a moment. "There is some benefit to me reducing the paper trail I leave down here, so not having to rent a place would be a good thing."

They are both quiet for several long minutes, each contemplating their next possible move. Finally Camden breaks the silence.

"I can't believe I'm saying this," she says, looking around the large space again, "but there is a second bedroom. There may be room for both of us. Perhaps."

Sal smiles and gives her a hug she struggles to extricate herself from. As they are leaving she looks around one last time. The apartment is filled with bookcases, but every one of them is empty.

"Don't you find it odd," she asks, "that there are no books in here?"

"Why would there be?" Sal answers. "He had an entire library downstairs."

Two hours later, Camden and Sal are sitting in the empty store. There is a pizza box on the counter. Sal drinks a beer and watches Camden's face for a clue to what's on her mind.

"So," he says, "what do you think?"

"I think I'm knackered," she says. "I think that we inherited a lunatic asylum. And I think my partner is probably the head lunatic."

"That's harsh. You barely know me."

"I know you tried to teach me how to hot-wire a car when I was 9 years old. Remember that?"

"It's a useful skill."

"I was nine! And it was at your Great Uncle Silvio's funeral."

"I was only 13," Sal says. "And Silvio would have been proud."

"I also think the only reason you're here is that things got too hot for you back home. Is your, ummm, Family in trouble?"

"The Family's fine. I'm the one who's got trouble."

"Right," she says. "A misunderstanding with someone's mother."

"For your information, cousin," he says, ignoring her comment, "I do love books. Books don't shoot at you, try to arrest you, or want a cut of the profits when you took all the risks. Books, and this store, are my ticket out of that life. Just like Frank said, the perverted old prophet."

When the beer is gone they make plans to meet early the next morning. On the way out, Sal grabs a copy of *A Moveable Feast* that sits atop a stack of books piled on a table.

"I'll walk you to your hotel," he tells her after locking the various bolts on the front door.

"No need. It's right on the corner there." She points down the block.

"Suit yourself. But these are mean streets."

"Right," she says with a grin.

He turns to leave, but Camden stops him.

"Since we're stuck together now," she says, "and since this is your new lease on life, do me a favor."

"What's that?"

"Stay off the causeway, Sonny."

He smiles, nods, and walks the opposite direction down the street to his car.

4

"The Phoenix Rises"

Much too early the next morning, Camden and Sal are in Franklin's office, a small cramped space with piles of papers, books, and unpaid invoices stacked everywhere. Camden is looking over a handwritten ledger, while Sal checks an inventory log. She puts down her pencil and lets out an audible sigh.

"How in the world did he keep this place open?" she asks. "Whoever compiled these accounts—Uncle Franklin, I assume—had the arithmetic skills of a kindergartener. And the handwriting looks suspiciously like Sanskrit."

"He didn't keep it open by trying to sell *these* books, that's for sure," Sal replies, flipping pages of the log. "They're great titles, no question, but maybe one person in a thousand would actually want them. And those people already own a copy. I detect Jacob's influence in some of these purchases."

"So in a word..."

"We're fucked."

"Quite," she says. "I was thinking something more along the lines of 'we need a plan to turn this ship around.'"

"That's a lot of words," he says, scribbling notes on the log sheets. "Mine was more to the point."

"Accurate as that assessment may be, it doesn't help us." She sits back in her chair. "Julia was right; everything needs to be changed. Why don't you go out and work on the inventory, and I'll sort through this mess and try to get a clearer picture of our finances."

"Fine with me. I need to check out which Sirens show up today anyway."

Camden rolls her eyes and looks down at another ledger as Sal walks to the office door.

"Enjoy it while you can," she says. "Our staffing model has to change too, and I think it will include far fewer Sirens."

"The English," he says, not turning around. "Crusading against sex since the time of Queen Victoria."

Julia is at the counter ringing up the lone customer in the shop. He has purchased an old volume of Tolstoy from Jacob, who smiles at Sal with smug satisfaction. The woman who handed him her number the night before sits on a small stool, polishing her nails. She looks up, blows him a kiss, then goes back to painting. She is apparently the Siren of the Day.

Julia hands the customer his change and walks over to Sal, who is looking at the front display window. The books are all short story collections by minor authors. He shakes his head at the selection.

"So, Jules, where would you start?"

"You want my honest opinion?"

"No sense in editing yourself now," he says with a smile.

"Total overhaul," she says with a confident nod. "*Total*. Get as many of the part-time ladies—"

"The Sirens?"

"Yes," she replies with an exasperated sigh, "the Sirens. Get as many of them in here to help as we can. Put computers where the cash register is, dump half the stock for whatever we can get for it, brighten the place up, and order some books written in this century."

"Not a fan of the classics?"

"Sal, I'd like nothing more than a world where everyone read Shakespeare and Jane Austen, but that's not the world I live in. And I have rent to pay."

"Still doesn't seem like enough to pack the place with customers."

"It's a start," she says, ideas obviously swirling around in her mind. "We also need to start hosting events, author signings, poetry readings...hell, even wine tastings. People still buy books today, but you have to be creative to get

47

them in the door instead of just buying online. Adding a kids' section would help too."

"That's quite a list," Sal says. *Seems like the only thing she wouldn't change is the name of the place*, he thinks.

"Oh, and we should change the name," she adds, almost as an afterthought.

"Change the name?" he asks, both shocked and wondering if she's a mind reader. "The place has been here for 50 years, and the name has too. How can we change it?"

"Easily," she says. "It's too formal, too stuffy. Everyone thinks Franklin Templeton Booksellers is an antiquarian, and thus *expensive*, store. That's why Jacob does most of the selling."

"I thought it was because he's an antique himself."

Julia laughs and nods. Camden strides up to them, clearly agitated. She holds a stack of papers.

"Julia, who handled the bills around here?"

"Mr. Templeton. He didn't trust anyone to write checks. It was a year before he would let me make the deposits."

Camden shows the stack of papers to Sal, her agitation growing by the minute.

"Look at this: Final Notices. The electricity will be shut off in two days, the phone in five, and the reason there are no new books is that the wholesalers haven't been paid in months. They've cut us off."

"So pay the bills," Sal says. "You're the accountant."

"The cash in the bank account won't come close to bringing all of these current, plus we have payroll coming up. And my personal savings is almost nil."

Julia shoots a worried look at Sal. He takes a cigarette from a pack in his pocket and lights it.

"What are you doing?!" Camden yells. "You can't smoke in here."

"I smoke while in deep thought. Chill out."

"Outside with that thing," she says, pointing to the door with her stack of bills. "Now."

"Fine, your majesty. Don't get your knickers in a knot."

As he heads for the front door, the lights in the store go out, leaving the room in darkness broken only by the sunlight streaming in through the front windows.

"Bollocks!" Camden exclaims.

"Guess you were off by a few days on the light bill," Sal says as the door closes behind him.

Within minutes the staff is gathered on the sidewalk in front of the shop. Sal smokes in silence while everyone else talks over each other. After a few moments he takes charge.

"Quiet, everybody," he says. "Here's what we'll do. Cam, get me a total of what absolutely has to be paid now to get the lights back on, keep the phone on, stuff like that. Julia, find out how much your computers and gizmos will cost, then get as many of the Sirens here as you can and start cleaning the place up."

"In the dark?" she asks.

"Hopefully by the time you get them here the lights will be back on. If not, improvise." He turns to Jacob. "Jacob, call any dealers you know who would buy any of this crap we don't need."

"Crap?" he repeats, indignant. "There is no crap in this store."

"Sure there is," Sal replies. "Loads of it. Get to shoveling or pack for Arizona."

"And what are you going to do?" Camden asks.

"I, my dear cousin, am going to do what I do best: get us the cash to pay for all of this."

"And how exactly do you propose to do that, unless you have a bank vault stashed somewhere and—"

She stops in mid-sentence and just stares at him. The others turn to him as well.

"No, I don't have a bank vault. I was in New Haven that night."

"Atlantic City," Julia reminds him.

"Right. But acquiring funds is my specialty. Trust me."

He gives them all a reassuring smile, walks to his car which is parked by the curb, and drives away.

The day is a whirlwind of activity, very little of it related in any way to actual bookselling. Camden writes checks while a Siren holds a flashlight over her, not even bothering to balance the checkbook as she goes. *At this point there's no money left, so no sense worrying about it,* she thinks to herself. *Either Sal will come through with the cash or he won't.*

At the front counter Julia is on the phone, which still works; thank God for old-fashioned landlines. She checks names off a list of employees as she dials. So far she has only tracked down two more of the Sirens. On the other side of the store, Jacob and Ramon sort through piles of books, occasionally disagreeing over what should stay and what should go.

"Mr. Sal said to get rid of as much as possible," Ramon says.

"Why aren't you in school?" Jacob asks, snatching a book from him.

"It's a teacher in-service day or some such nonsense," Ramon says. "They're probably sitting around drinking coffee and complaining about what idiots their students are. Now about that book..."

"We need this copy," Jacob insists.

"There are three identical copies."

"Never hurts to have back-stock," Jacob says without much conviction.

"I have heard there are no trees over five feet tall in the whole state of Arizona," Ramon says, a gleam in his eye. "Is that true?"

Jacob doesn't answer. He simply stares at Ramon, then at the book, and slowly hands it over. Ramon smiles and puts it in a box.

Across town, Sal drives down a residential street filled with McMansions, making notes as he passes each one. He stops in front of one, puts on an Atlantic Bell Telephone hardhat and leather tool belt he retrieves from his trunk, then walks to the back of the house. He returns a few minutes later, counting a stack of bills as he gets into his car.

Just after noon, Julia drives Camden to the electric company office. Cam gestures wildly over the bill for several minutes, then relents and hands a wad of cash to the clerk. After she counts out the bills, she looks in her wallet to see what remains: two fives and a one. When they return to the store, Ramon hands her an envelope.

"From Mr. Sal," he says. "He gave it to me and left again."

She opens the envelope; it is filled with cash. She doesn't know where it came from, though she can certainly guess. She looks at the money for a moment, unsure what to do. Then she hands the envelope to Julia.

"You said you've done the deposits before," Camden says. "Let's get this in the bank."

Late that night, Sal's car sits a block away from a closed jewelry store. He emerges from the darkness of the alley behind the store, holding a large bag in his hand. He is smiling like a kid at Christmas. He walks casually to his car, gets in, and drives away.

The next few days are more of the same. Ramon washes the front windows while a Siren holds the ladder and inspects her nails. Jacob boxes up books and takes cash from a man, who then loads them onto a dolly as Jacob shakes his head sadly. Julia makes signs for the new genre sections using small chalkboards and colored chalk.

Back in the office, Camden pores over more handwritten ledgers and writes out more checks. At one point she stops and bangs her head on the desk. Sal enters and hands her a stack of one-hundred dollar bills, then immediately leaves. This time she doesn't hesitate; she pulls out a deposit slip and calls Julia.

Late in the day, Ramon installs new lights while a different Siren holds the ladder. She also inspects her nails. Julia shows yet a different Siren how to work the new computers that have just been delivered. It is not an easy task. Ramon and some friends he has recruited from school move bookcases from one part of the store to another, then back again. The scene repeats itself as Jacob argues with Cam and Julia over the size of the antiquarian section.

By the fifth day, the store has risen from the dead. It looks completely different, and they have even received the first of several orders of new books from publishers, having requested and paid for overnight shipping. Finally, a new sign specially designed by Julia goes up over the front of the shop. It reads: *The Last Word.*

5

"Now Hiring"

After a thorough review, it is clear that Camden and Julia were right: the staffing model that Franklin loved so much was part of what drove the bookstore to the brink of insolvency. Twenty-seven come-when-you-feel-like-it part-time employees was simply no way to run a business, no matter how beautiful or gifted in the bedroom arts they might be. In the end Sal and Camden, with input from Julia, decide to keep the four most capable of the Sirens. They all have names, of course, but Sal designates them Siren One, Siren Two, Siren Three, and Siren Four. Not original, but consistent with his late uncle's love of Greek mythology. Siren One, it turns out, has a very unusual knowledge base, as they learned one morning when a customer came in asking if they had any baseball trivia books.

"What exactly do you need to know?" Sal asked.

"Who hit the most home runs in 1968?" the customer replied.

"Which league, American or National?" Siren One responded, not looking up from the nail she was buffing.

"National," he said.

"Willie McCovey, San Francisco Giants," she replied without hesitation.

The customer nodded quickly, thanked them, then dashed out of the store. Sal stared at her, amazed.

"How did you know that?" he asked.

"I was an only child," she answered. "And my dad was a baseball fanatic. Granddad too. It was inevitable."

"I see," Sal answered. "And just for my own knowledge, in case it comes up during a game of Trivial Pursuit or something, the American League home run champ for '68 was…"

"Frank Howard, Washington Senators," she said immediately.

"Good to know."

Keeping the four Sirens still left the shop with only four full-time employees plus Ramon, who seemed to be there as much as he was in school, and they needed at least one more. So on a rainy Monday morning a simple sign— elegantly drawn in colored chalk on a small, square, framed blackboard—was hung in the front window: Now Hiring. Ads were placed and resumes reviewed (new territory for both Sal and Camden) and finally a day was set aside for interviews.

The morning the interviews are to take place, Sal and Camden are sorting through a box of books. Sal examines each one, tells Camden a price, and she writes it on the front flyleaf of the book.

"I hope to God these interviews pan out," he says. "We've got to have some help around here before Julia quits and leaves us alone with Jacob."

"I just hope we have at lot of good applicants to choose from," she replies, a tad too optimistically in Sal's opinion. "And that we choose the right one."

"At this point I'd hire a chimp if he could sort books and not crap on the floor."

"I can't believe I'm saying this," Camden says, "but you worry too much sometimes."

"That's what you underpay me for."

Later in the morning they are seated in the small break room, Sal looking over a resume and Camden chatting amiably with a professionally dressed female applicant. Sal glances up at the wall clock, which reads 9:15 am.

"I'm very good at spreadsheets," the woman says. "Formulas, pivot tables, you name it. I can handle any spreadsheet you might need."

"Well, we're a bookstore," Camden replies. "We don't have much need for spreadsheets here."

"Everyone needs spreadsheets, dear."

Sal looks from the woman to Camden and forces a smile. He turns the woman's resume over, face-down, on the table.

A few minutes later, Sal is looking at another application. He asks a question of the next job seeker, a woman in her early twenties.

"Any hobbies?"

"Hmm...would stripping count as a hobby? I just started this week and haven't gotten my first check yet."

Sal looks at Camden and his eyes brighten. She slaps him in the back of the head, and he places this application face-down as well.

The next applicant is a casually dressed man in his mid-30s. Camden decides to take a different approach.

"Let's start with something simple," she says. "Who wrote *Great Expectations*?"

The man ponders this for far too long before answering.

"I can't remember the lady's name," he finally says, "but I know she also wrote *What to Expect When You're Expecting*. I think *Great Expectations* was the sequel."

Sal is unable to contain himself and laughs out loud. Camden gives him a sharp look and he regains his composure, then adds another resume to the "no" pile. He has higher hopes for the next guy, a small man in his 20s who at least looks like someone who has read a book.

"What do Saramago, Zafon, Garcia-Marquez, and Carlos Fuentes have in common?"

"I'm pretty sure that's the infield for the Boston Red Sox. I know Fuentes plays shortstop. Although Zafon may have been traded to Cleveland for a relief pitcher."

Camden snorts and crosses the young man's name off a list. This is going to be much harder than either of them expected. The next applicant is in his late teens, barely out of high school.

"What would you say is the most poorly-written bestseller of all time?" Camden asks him.

"The Bible, hands down. With all those begats and thees and thous I don't see how anyone can read the thing. It's like it was written in the 1600s or something. You'd think Jesus could write better than that."

Camden drops her face into her hands. The clock on the wall shows noon. Julia ushers in the next applicant, a young woman about her age. Sal takes the chance that she remembers something from her college English classes.

"Name three of the Lost Generation writers," he says.

"If they're lost then how am I supposed to name them?" she asks, without a hint of irony. "Look, it's not like this job is rocket science. Can't I just blow you instead of answering these stupid questions? I've gotten lots of jobs that way."

Sal looks hopefully at Camden, his eyebrows raised. She shakes her head "no," but at least she doesn't slap him this time.

They take a short break for lunch, hopeful things will get better in the afternoon. Maybe the really good candidates sleep late, or have morning classes, or something. Anything.

The first interviewee of the afternoon is an older woman wearing a *Little House on the Prairie* dress and a large cross on a chain.

"Who wrote *Of Human Bondage* and *The Razor's Edge?*" Camden asks her.

"Probably the same pervert who wrote those *50 Shades of Grey* books—LeBron James," the woman answers. "I'm not into bondage or cutting or any of that sick nonsense. And I don't think a reputable bookseller should carry those books. Pornography should not be out in the open. It should be in places where children can't get to it, like the Internet."

"Actually," Sal says, "LeBron James is a professional basketball player."

"I'm not surprised," the woman says. "They're all degenerates."

Sal bangs his head on the desk repeatedly until Julia comes in and shows the lady out. The next applicant is a huge bearded man who could easily have just arrived after a year living in the Yukon.

"So why do you want to work in a bookstore?" Sal asks him, deciding on a question that really could have no wrong answer.

"I don't like people very much," the bearded giant replies, "but I do like to eat, as you can see. This requires that I have a job, and unfortunately most jobs involve being around people. I don't think the Kindle or Amazon will ever completely wipe out bookstores or real books, but they'll diminish enough that working here I should only have to deal with a handful of people a day. Most of those will either be tech-ignorant or tech-hostile, and probably not very talkative or outgoing, so I can just sit around and get paid to read and ring up the occasional purchase from a quiet recluse. Everybody wins."

Sal and Camden both stare at him, speechless. Camden places his application in the "no" pile, along with everyone else they have interviewed today. The clock is at 4:00 pm.

"How many more do we have?" she asks.

"Just one. I told you this was gonna be a beating. Bring her in and let's get it over with."

Camden leaves the break room to get the last applicant while Sal wearily examines the woman's application. Cam returns with Heather Morrison, a girl of nineteen or twenty with multiple piercings and even more tattoos. The girl slumps down in the chair. Sal decides to get this over with quickly so he can start drinking this miserable day away.

"If a woman came in and asked you for a copy of *50 Shades of Grey*, what would you tell her?"

"I'd tell her she should read *Madame Bovary* instead," Heather replies. "It leaves more to the imagination and it wasn't written by an illiterate hack."

Sal smiles. Sylvia looks up from Heather's application.

"I might also recommend Dan Brown," Heather continues, "though the customer would likely have read all his books already. He's amazing."

Sal's smile quickly fades, and Camden shakes her head sadly. Heather starts to laugh.

"Just messing with you," she says. "I wouldn't even wrap dead fish in pages from a Dan Brown novel. It's disrespectful to the fish."

Sal and Camden are both laughing now. They seem relaxed for the first time in hours.

"One last question," Sal says. "What novel is Hemingway best known for?"

"All of them," Heather immediately replies. "Hemingway was a genius. After struggling valiantly, all his characters die. Alone. In the rain. Which is kinda cool."

Sal and Camden look at each other, then at Heather, then back at each other. They nod and reply in unison.

"You're hired."

"Awesome," she says. "No more working at Target for me. Hey, can I ask you a question?"

Sal braces himself for another Ithaca-related query. Camden is apparently expecting the same, and relishing Sal's discomfort.

"Certainly," Cam says. "We're just one big dysfunctional family here."

"I imagine you've had a lot of girls from TCU apply," Heather says. It's more of a statement than a question.

"Actually yes," Sal replies. "More than I expected. I thought there would be more stay-at-home moms who were tired of, well, staying at home."

"How many of them offered to have sex with you to get the job?" she asks. "The students, not the moms. Well, maybe the moms too." It is definitely a question.

"There were a few offers of... *favors* would be the word, I guess," Sal answers.

"Favors," she repeats. "So they mainly offered blow jobs." She smiles wickedly when she says this.

"Right," Sal says. Camden is not enjoying the direction this is going, but Sal clearly is.

"Hire any of them?"

"No," Camden says firmly. "Is there a reason you're asking about this?"

"Just curious about my competition," she says. "If those little rich girls ever had to work at Target during the holidays, they might have offered to do more."

"You're not saying—" Sal replies, "—and I cannot believe I am asking this, you're not saying you would have made the same offer?"

"Would you have accepted if I had?"

"Absolutely not."

"I figured that," Heather says with a nod. "That's why I'll take the job."

"Strong ethical standards, I see," Camden says a little sarcastically.

"Something like that. And just out of curiosity," she says, turning directly to Sal again, "are you as strict about non-fraternization with employees as with applicants?"

"I'm not sure," he says. "I've never had employees before. Maybe, and maybe not."

Camden gives them both a horrified look.

"So you're not a pig," Heather says, "and you're not a Puritan. I like that in a boss, and in a man." She licks her lips, then stands and shakes their hands. "So I start tomorrow, right?"

"Tomorrow will be fine," Camden says, glad the conversation is over. But it isn't.

"Cool," she says, then turns to leave. Her hand is already on the doorknob when she stops and turns back to Sal.

"Just so you know," she says, "I'm not the kind of girl who would offer oral sex just to get a job."

"I didn't think you were," he replies.

"But if we were ever to end up in the fiction section alone, on a rainy night, and you happened to be reading aloud from *A Farewell to Arms*…well, consider yourself forewarned."

When she is gone, Sal turns to Camden, who is still too stunned to speak.

"I've said it before," he says, "and I'll say it again. I think I'm gonna like it here. No doubt about it."

6

"Welcome to the Neighborhood"

Sal is inexplicably edgy. He has already argued with a deliveryman, snapped at Jacob, and glared at a long-browsing customer until the man became uncomfortable and left the store. It is not yet noon.

"What is wrong with you today?" Camden finally asks, the only one brave enough to approach him in his current foul mood.

"Nothing."

"Obviously," she says. "Spill it, Terranova."

He tries to glare at her as had the customer, but cannot hold it. His shoulders sag and he lets out a breath.

"I feel disconnected here," he says so softly she almost doesn't hear him.

"Disconnected? What does that mean? You mean from us?" She looks a little hurt as she says it.

"No," he says, glancing around to be sure only she can hear him. "From the place, the neighborhood."

He is quiet for a moment, and Julia remains silent herself; it is clear he wants to say more and is just searching for the right words.

"I'm a city kid," he finally continues, "and I've always felt, I don't know, in tune with my neighborhood. I knew the people, the places, knew immediately when something or someone didn't belong. I don't have that here."

"Then get to know it here," Cam says firmly, "and get out of this funk." She looks across the store at Jacob. "Jacob, would you show Sal around downtown? I think a nice stroll will make him feel less edgy."

"I do not stroll around downtown, young lady," he replies stiffly. "At my age I rarely stroll anywhere. Why don't you take him? He is your cousin, after all."

"But I don't know this area any better than he does," she protests. "Heather, how about you?"

"Nope," she says. "I do everything by car, and I don't live down here. Now, if he wants to drive around the Berry Street/University area, I could do that."

Camden looks inquisitively at Sal, who shakes his head.

"It's not this neighborhood, so it's not the same," he says.

"Would you really call this a neighborhood?" Siren Three asks. "It's mainly offices and shops."

"It is most definitely a neighborhood," Sal says firmly. "People live here too. *I* live here. This separation between where you live, work and shop that exists in this state is unnatural, and it's why everyone has to drive everywhere, even to get a quart of milk or a loaf of bread. It's nuts."

"For crying out loud," Julia says, joining the conversation. "I'll show you around if it will improve your surly mood. I also live down here."

Sal ponders this for a moment, and then indicates his agreement with the slightest nod of his head. Camden breathes a sigh of relief, mainly because now she won't have to go with him.

"We can take a long lunch," Julia continues, but Sal immediately shakes his head.

"Too hot," he says. "I hate to sweat."

"It's summer in Texas, Sal," Camden says, ready for this to just be over. "It's going to be hot until September."

"November," Heather corrects her.

"Just meet me in front of the shop tomorrow at 7 a.m.," Julia says. "It should be cool enough then for your delicate constitution."

Sal hates early mornings almost as much as he hates to sweat, but he is waiting outside when Julia arrives the following day. He hands her a large coffee and a blueberry muffin from Kate's Bakery.

"I know you like the raspberry better," he says, "but they were sold out already."

She thanks him and takes the coffee and muffin, making a mental note that he has remembered raspberry is her favorite. She looks up and down the block, trying to decide which direction to begin this magical mystery walking tour, finally heading southeast on Third Street. She wishes they were closer to the cultural district, with the Kimball and the Museum of Science and History, but knows that not only would Sal never walk that far since it is technically not part of his "neighborhood," he probably doesn't like museums anyway. Not manly enough for a gangster, even a former one.

"I expected you to try to switch this little excursion to the evening," she says as they cross Main Street. "You're not much of an early riser."

"I thought about it," he says, closely inspecting each building they pass, "but it's not the same at night. Too many tourists, too many people from other parts of town. I need a feel for the soul of the place, not the pretty face it shows to outsiders."

"I see," she says, not really sure that she does. She has lived here for two years and never once given a thought to the soul of the place.

"So how long have you lived down here?" Sal asks, causing her to wonder briefly if he can read her thoughts. *Obviously not*, she thinks.

"Two years."

"Where did you live before? Are you a native Texan, or a carpetbagger like me?"

"Definitely not a carpetbagger," she says with a laugh. "I grew up in the Wedgewood area; that's in southwest Fort Worth. I graduated from Southwest High school."

"But you know downtown, right?" he asks.

"Sure," she replies.

They walk for a few blocks, with Julia pointing out things she thinks will interest him. There are a lot of restaurants, some trendy boutiques, and several nightclubs. Each time she describes a location, Sal simply nods or says "uh huh." She finally stops on the sidewalk in front of a Bagel Boys bagel shop. He is not paying attention and walks on several steps before realizing she is not beside him. He turns around and walks back to her.

"Why'd you stop?" he asks.

"Because I don't really think you're listening to me," she says a little more defensively than she intends.

"Sure I am," he says. "The last two blocks we've passed a frozen yogurt place, a Mongolian grill, a blues bar, an Italian restaurant I bet serves food that barely resembles Italian, a shop that sells vintage clothing at ten times what it cost back when it was new, a police substation, and a Thomas Kincaide art gallery. You said you like ice cream more than frozen yogurt, like jazz more than blues, and think Thomas Kincaide is kitsch." After he says all this, she stares at him in astonishment.

"Wow," she says. "You just didn't seem all that interested."

"I'm interested," he says reassuringly, "and you are a great tour guide. But I'm also looking for something else."

"What?"

"The flow," he says, as if this explains everything. She gives him a blank stare. "Okay, sit down and let me explain." He motions to an empty bench near a corner and they take a seat. He lights a cigarette before continuing. "The buildings, stores, and whatnot are all important. The *people* are just as important. Like that guy running down the street," he motions to a man jogging away from them. "Does he run at the same time every morning, or is he businessman from out of town who likes to keep a normal routine even when he travels? And the old man sweeping in front of the bagel shop—is he the owner or an employee? Does that cop on the bicycle over there like to break people's balls because he's on a power trip, or is he really looking out for the neighborhood? And is he embarrassed about riding a bike?"

"That's the flow?" she asks, starting to understand a little better.

"That's the flow. Now I'm gonna have to come out here at this time every day for a while to see what the pattern is. Then I'll know when something is out of whack."

"Out of whack?" she repeats.

"Yeah. Like that homeless guy we passed a block back."

72

"You are not going to start going off about how the homeless just need to get off drugs, get a job and work harder, are you?" she interrupts.

"Uh, no," he says. "I was actually going to say that I will be shocked if he's here when I come back tomorrow. That guy's not homeless."

She turns and looks back up the block. She can just make out the man, sitting on the sidewalk with his back against a wall. He definitely looks homeless.

"What makes you say that?" she asks, still looking in the man's direction.

"His shoes," Sal says. "The soles look new. When you're on the street the first thing that wears out is your shoes. The clothes appear right, but too right, like they were chosen specifically for that look. And although his face has dirt smudged on it, his hair was clearly washed in the past day. At best it should be the other way around."

"Why would he be impersonating a homeless man?" Julia asks, intrigued by how Sal noticed all of this just walking by the man. "For money?"

"I don't think so," he says, shaking his head. "There wasn't even a cup or anything near him to throw coins in. If I had to guess, I'd say he's a cop working undercover, watching someone."

Now she is very interested, which he should have expected from someone who watches Crime TV regularly.

"Who do you think he's watching?" She says this almost whispering, as if the guy can hear them from a block away.

"No clue," he replies, flicking his cigarette into the gutter and standing up. "I don't know the flow yet, remember, so there's no way to even guess." He starts walking again, and she hurries to catch up.

"Where did you learn to do that? I mean, how did you size that guy up so quickly?"

"Lots of practice, I guess. Back home, neighborhoods are a lot more insular than here; each one is its own self-contained world. Outsiders are usually only there to cause trouble of some kind, so we notice them. It will be harder to read things here because of the tourists, like I said earlier, but I think it will come with time."

He stops again at Oak Street between Fifth and Sixth Streets; this block seems different from the rest, older and more run-down. In fact, the row of buildings looks even older than the building that houses the bookshop.

"What's the story here?" he asks. "No shiny new shops or offices on this block."

"No," she says. "There is a fight between the developers and the historical preservationists over this block. These buildings are among the oldest in the city. People say that Butch Cassidy actually lived in that one for a while." She points at a crumbling brownstone that would have been more at home in his old neighborhood in Trenton than this one. "Some even say it's haunted."

"Haunted," he repeats. "I like that. It's good to have a ghost or two around, to keep things lively." He stops in front of the last empty storefront in the row, a smile spreading across his face. "That," he says, "was a bookstore."

"Yep," she says. It's impressive that he knows this, since there is no outward sign of what type of store it once was. "And they say there are still books in there."

"Really? I just may have to check that out. I'm fairly certain I can get in." His smile broadens, and Julia hustles him quickly away before she becomes an accessory to whatever crime he has in mind.

They walk on for another block, finally stopping at a place called the Daily Grind near Commerce and 5th Street to replenish their coffee. Next door is a large resale shop, and though it is not open yet, Sal can see books through the window.

"Think there are any good books in there?" he asks.

"Sometimes," she answers. "Jacob used to come down here about once a month to see if they've accidentally stumbled upon something we could sell. Now he just waits for Eli to call him."

"Who is Eli?"

"He works here. If he finds something Jacob wants he buys it himself, then sells it to us for a little profit. He's a strange guy though. He likes to leaf through our used books looking for stuff."

"What kind of stuff?"

"Letters, photographs, anything someone might have used as a bookmark and forgotten about when they sold the books. I think he collects them."

"It takes all kinds, I guess," Sal says. "If he gets us some good books occasionally he can look for all the bookmarks he wants." He glances at his watch and realizes it is close to 9:00 a.m. "The store will be open soon," he says. "We should probably head back." Before she can answer he pulls her across the street, ignoring a 'Don't Walk' signal as they go.

In front of the shop again, Sal looks out over his immediate domain, and appears to like what he sees. The edginess isn't completely gone, but it is lessened considerably.

"Thanks for the tour, Jules. Maybe next week we can cross the river and check out some of the museums I hear are over there. The museums are one of the things I miss most about being close to New York and Philly. And the food, of course."

"That sounds fun," she says, surprised and pleased at the same time.

7

"The Day the Shop Stood Still"

The store is buzzing with activity prior to opening, in no small part because it is Tuesday, the day new releases arrive from the publishers. These new releases are all arranged on tables at the front, but Camden is suddenly not happy with one of the displays and frantically rearranges it—with Julia's help—before allowing customers in. Jacob is also rearranging his section, moving some Russian novels out of a locked case at the back of the rare books area to a smaller locked case closer to the front. Sal looks inquisitively at him.

"Is it Stalin's birthday?" he asks. "Or maybe the anniversary of the Battle of Kursk?"

"I don't think it's either," Jacob answers. "Why?"

"I thought there might actually be a reason you're moving all the dead Russians up front."

"Just a feeling I've got," he answered. "When you've been in the trade as long as I have, you get a feeling about this sort of thing."

"I see." Sal barely contains a laugh. "You've got a feeling that someone is going to get a sudden urge for a first edition Tolstoy or a signed *Gulag Archipelago*. Remind me to take you to the track next time I go....you can pick my horses for me."

Camden looks over at the two them and frowns.

"Sal," she says with an irritated voice, "stop harassing Jacob and go unlock the doors. Please."

He bows and walks to the front door.

"I live to serve, your majesty," he says as he passes her.

He unlocks the door and holds it open for the customers who are waiting outside. No one enters. He steps out and looks up and down the street. Nothing.

"There's no one out there," he says upon re-entering the shop. "Street's empty, too."

Camden looks at him as if he's just said that giant wheels of cheese were rolling down the street.

"What do you mean empty?" she asks, hurrying to the door herself. "The street can't be empty."

But it is. There are a few cars parked in their normal spots, but not a single human in sight. She goes back inside.

"This is very odd," she says to no one in particular.

"You're all a bunch of rookies," Jacob says with a snort. "Sometimes they're waiting, and sometimes they're not.

But the customers will come. It's new-release Tuesday, after all."

"Right," adds Sal. "Plus, the great-great-great-grandson of Ivan the Terrible will be by any minute to snatch up a copy of *Anna Karenina*."

Jacob starts to answer, but just shakes his head and walks back to his section of the shop. Seeing a rare opportunity, Siren One speaks up.

"Since we're slow right now, maybe I could take my break early and run over to the nail salon? I really need a manicure."

Sal looks at Julia, who simply smiles and gives him a thumbs-up.

Two hours later there has still not been a single customer. This has caused the staff (including Siren One, who has returned from her manicure) to begin speculating on what the cause could be.

"The Rapture," Siren One says, admiring her nails. "Definitely the Rapture."

"I didn't know you were evangelical," Julia says.

"I'm not exactly sure what that means," she answers gravely, "but I did read most of that series of books about the Rapture. I hope I wasn't left behind...it's gonna be ugly."

Camden stares at her; she is not joking.

"I think it's the Horse Latitudes," Julia says. "Like those sailors in the 16th century who had to throw their horses overboard to get the wind to blow again."

Camden turns her attention to Julia. A wink tells her that Julia definitely *is* joking.

"Maybe it's because the books being published today are crap," Jacob says. "I wouldn't come in for those either. Now if people read more Russian novelists…"

Camden doesn't even bother to look at him.

"I thought you said we were all a bunch of rookies and that the customers would come," Sal says.

"They will," Jacob answers with a slight smile. "Eventually. But I stand by my earlier statements."

"Your earlier statements take both sides…hard to ever be wrong that way."

"Age has its privileges."

"Look!" Julia exclaims, stopping their banter. She points at the door.

They all turn and see a middle-aged man at the front door. As he is about to push the door open, he looks through the glass and sees everyone staring at him. He hesitates, then quickly turns and hurries away. A collective, exasperated sigh is heard in the shop.

A few hours later, Sal and Julia are having lunch at a burger joint that is *not* lacking in customers. Julia drinks tea; Sal orders another beer. Two empty bottles are already in front of him.

"If you go back drunk, Camden will be mad," she points out in a pleasant tone. He is one of the bosses after all.

"Who cares? It's not like we have any customers."

"We will," she says almost defensively. "They won't stay away the entire day."

Sal looks at his watch: it is 1:15.

"They're doing a good job so far." He eats some of his fries, then has an idea. "Hey, do you think Randy's store has been empty all day too?"

She ponders this for a moment.

"I suppose it's possible. Do you want to go by and check?"

"Yes. Wait…no. We'd have to go inside to be sure, and once we're inside we will have caused him to have customers. Damn it."

"Wow, three beers at lunch really doesn't impair your ability to think things through," she says admiringly.

"Not one bit, angel."

He winks, and Julia quickly looks away before her face flushes red.

"I know one thing," he continues. "We need a seriously kick-ass plan to get customers in the door or all the renovations in the world won't matter one bit."

Late that afternoon someone finally enters the shop. Unfortunately it is the postman delivering a package. Like much of the correspondence they receive, it is still addressed to Franklin Templeton. Sal opens the box and removes a shrink-wrapped stack of labels. The top label is visible; it has an odd-looking crest, and the words:

Ex Libris
Franklin Templeton.

"What the heck is this?" he asks Jacob, who has just walked up to see if it might be an autographed book he's waiting on.

"What is it?" Jacob repeats, incredulous. "I thought you knew books, son. Those are bookplates. 'Ex Libris' means 'from the library of' Franklin Templeton."

"I know they're bookplates, Jacob," Sal says sharply, "and I know what 'Ex Libris' means. But why did Uncle Frank need them?"

"For his books, of course. Why else? Heck, you live in his apartment. You've seen his books."

"There are no books in his apartment. Camden commented on it the first night we were here, but I figured he just saw the store as his own personal collection."

"Now that's very odd," Jacob says. "He had a good collection. Nothing flashy, but quite good. Where could they have gone?"

"I don't know," Sal replies. "But I'm going to find out."

8

"And a Child Shall Lead Them"

Camden is sitting at the counter on a Saturday morning, engaged in her favorite activity: balancing the accounts. She doesn't miss her London firm at all—the bloody ferrets—but she still loves numbers. Numbers are straightforward, reliably consistent, and rarely turn out to be homosexual after several years of marriage. She is about to move on to the dreaded profit and loss statement when a small voice interrupts her train of thought.

"Excuse me, ma'am," the voice says.

Cam looks up from her laptop to see a young girl, not yet a teenager, standing at the counter. She is holding a copy of *Harry Potter and the Sorcerer's Stone*. Camden still does not understand why the American publishers changed the original title from *Harry Potter and the Philosopher's Stone* (as it had been published in England) to this *Sorcerer's Stone* nonsense. What the hell was a Sorcerer's Stone, anyway?

"Would you like to buy that book?" Camden asks her sweetly.

"Oh, no," the girl answers, her voice not as soft as before. "I have the whole series at home."

"I see. Are you looking for more books about wizards, then?"

"No, I've actually moved on to Faulkner," the girl says proudly. Heather is standing nearby and, overhearing this last comment, walks over and joins them.

"Then what exactly can I help you with, young lady?" Camden asks, wishing Heather would take over this conversation.

"I was wondering about the way you shelve the Harry Potter books," the girl says.

"Shelve them?"

"Yes. What I mean is, why are all of them in the children's section?"

At this point Heather attempts to rescue Camden from the pint-sized inquisitor.

"Hi," she says. "I'm Heather. What's your name?"

"Sophia," the girl answers. "My name is the Greek word for wisdom. You can call me Sophie, though; only my Nana calls me Sophia."

"It's very nice to meet you Sophie," Heather says. "How old are you?"

"Eleven," she replies. "I'll be twelve in four months."

"And you're reading Faulkner?" Camden exclaims. The girl nods.

"I was reading Hemingway when I was nine," Heather says, more to the girl than to Camden. "You want to know why we put the Potter books in the children's section, you say? The main reason is that they are classified as being for readers ages 9 to 12 years old. And it's usually children who ask for them. I know some stores put books 4 through 7 in a separate Young Adult section, but we haven't done that here. I like keeping the whole series together."

The girl nods politely. Camden looks back at her computer, and Heather starts to turn away.

"I think you're wrong," the girl says, sounding more instructive than accusatory. Camden looks up again and Heather stops.

"Wrong?" Heather asks. "Why?"

"Because," Sophie says, but then she is distracted by Heather's arm, which she notices for the first time. "Is that Bugs Bunny holding a book?" she asks.

Heather smiles and looks down at the tattoo on the inside of her left forearm. She holds it out for Sophie to look at more closely. It is indeed Bugs Bunny, wearing a floppy hat and holding a copy of *The Old Man and the Sea*.

"Like it?" she asks.

"It's awesome," Sophie says. "Mom won't let me get a tattoo until I'm older. Anyway, the reason I think you're wrong to shelve Harry Potter just in the children's section is that they're not just books for kids."

"I agree that it's not simply children's literature," Heather says, "especially the later books. But where would you put them, if not where we have them now?

"Everywhere."

"Everywhere?" Camden says. "We can't possibly put every book in every section of the store. That would be the same as having no sections at all."

The girl stares at her, frustrated that she is not getting her point across.

"I don't mean every book, ma'am," she says. "But some books should be shelved that way, and Harry Potter is one of them. You already do it with Alice."

"Alice?" Heather asks.

"*Alice in Wonderland*," Sophie replies. "You have it in the children's section, and also in the fiction section. There's even an expensive copy over where that older man who looks like my grandpa is standing." She motions toward Jacob. "He tries to seem mean, but he winked at me and made a silly face when no one was looking. So that's three different sections for the same book."

"The little lady has a point," says Sal, who has walked over to them. "I could hear most of the conversation from where I was trying to doze over by the history section and I thought I'd come help even the odds."

"Even the odds?" Camden asks. "So you agree with her?"

"I do agree with her," he says with a nod. "But evening the odds means helping you and Heather out, since you're so obviously overmatched by a pre-teen."

Heather starts to protest, but Sal holds up his hand, stopping her.

"Camden, where do we shelve the Tolkien books?" he asks.

"In science fiction & fantasy," she replies.

"*The Hobbit's* also in the children's section," Heather says.

"How about C.S. Lewis's *Narnia* series?"

"Also sci-fi/fantasy?" Her reply is more of a question.

"And the children's area," Heather says.

"And the Christian Fiction section," Jacob adds, joining them.

"Right," he says. "So we have at least three authors whose books are spread throughout the store. Why is Miss Sophie here wrong about Potter?"

"You want to hear an old man's opinion?" Jacob asks.

They all turn to look at him. Camden fears he's going to start attacking the declining standards of literature; Sal is not so sure. Sophie gazes hopefully at him, probably because he looks like her grandpa.

"J.K. Rowling's tale of a boy wizard has held the world spellbound for more than fifteen years now," Jacob begins, "and done it while using story elements so ingrained in our collective memory that readers were amazed by the freshness of it. Albus Dumbledore may be the greatest wizard of all time (no offense to Gandalf), but when it comes to weaving a magical tale, he doesn't come close to his creator.

"The good versus evil storyline has existed since the beginning of time," he continues, looking particularly at Camden. "In fact, it's ultimately the basis of most of the world's religions. Stories of magic have existed almost as long, and the story of the orphan who overcomes great odds was popularized by Charles Dickens more than 150 years ago. Yet Rowling took these well-known elements and through a gifted literary alchemy produced something both familiar and new at the same time."

"Preach it," Sophie says, then quickly adds, "that's what we say at my church when the pastor gets on a roll."

Jacob smiles at this, then pauses for a moment to ensure he has everyone's attention. He does, including that of several customers, Sophie's mother among them. No one seems bored by his speech, though he would have continued on regardless.

"Harry Potter himself could have easily been a one-dimensional character, the lone hero forced to confront the greatest evil the world has ever know. Frodo in *The Lord of the Rings* is such a character, never really growing or maturing during the journey, simply putting one foot in front of the other. But Rowling did something with Harry and the rest of the young characters that hadn't been done before in children's literature: she let them grow up. Harry is 11 years old when we meet him, downtrodden by the Dursely's and unaware of his magical abilities. Over the next seven years he grows in the same way any child does, through trial and error, having goods days and bad—sometimes very, very bad—and discovering who he is as a person, a friend, and a reluctant hero."

Sal moves closer to Camden and whispers in her ear.

"Who would have thought the old dude who loves dead Russians was an expert on Harry Potter?"

"The other characters, particularly Ron Weasley and Hermione Granger, also develop and grow throughout the series," Jacob continues, "and the romantic tension between them in the later books was yet another twist on 'typical' children's literature. Rowling also makes the stories and characters real by having them deal with death in virtually every book. Death is a subject that rarely receives thoughtful consideration even in adult fiction, yet Rowling tackles it from the first chapter of *Harry Potter and the Sorcerer's Stone*."

He looks down at Sophie, who nods in agreement. He goes on.

"The way Rowling portrays the adults in the series is yet another surprising piece of magic," he says. "In most children's books, adults are either not present at all or are little more than bumbling idiots for the kids to outwit."

"Like how there are never any parents around in the Charlie Brown cartoons?" a customer asks. "Except for that teacher no one can understand?"

Exactly like that," Jacob says. "The adults in the Harry Potter books are fully formed characters whose stories could stand alone if you removed the kids entirely. Rowling shows us the adults' strengths and flaws, glories and failures, and she does it from the perspective of the students in most cases; what they—and we—learn about Dumbledore, Sirius Black, Lupin, Snape, and others comes out slowly over the course of the narrative. And, as in life, sometimes the kids seem more grown up than the adults, and sometimes it's the other way around."

Jacob pauses to take a sip of his coffee. He is near the end and wants to finish strong. For some reason it is suddenly important to him that his new bookselling family see him as more than just a peddler of old Russian novels. And he agrees with Sophie, too.

"None of these things, however, would make the Potter books the best-selling series of all time, with 400 million copies sold in over 30 languages and still growing, if Rowling hadn't also written an amazingly compelling page-turner of a series. That it is both a great beach read and truly literature at the same time is all the more remarkable. She has woven the best parts of the hero-quest, magical fantasy, romance, Gothic suspense, social commentary, and even detective fiction into a tapestry that looks like nothing we'd ever seen before.

"J.K. Rowling may not be able to turn lead into gold," he says, "but getting both a generation of kids *and* their parents to put down the PlayStation and TV remote long enough to read a tale that spans seven books and more than 4,000 pages is an even more remarkable feat of alchemy. She is without a doubt the greatest magician in the literary world. So, as to the question of what section Harry Potter belongs in, I say the young lady here is right. He belongs in all of them: kids, young adult, fantasy, religion, and most especially literature."

He takes another sip of coffee and waits for a rebuttal; there is none. How could there be? Instead everyone in the store applauds. And it is real applause, not sarcastic, Eddie Haskel applause. Sophie rushes over and hugs him.

"Well said," Sal says.

"You surprised me," Heather says, "and I don't surprise easily. I was afraid at first that you might take off on some religious fanatic screed about witches and the devil."

"Well," Jacob says with a gleam in his eye, "you would have gotten a screed if the question had been about that *Twilight* series, but not because I object to books about the powers of darkness. I object to books that are poorly written. And to changing 500 years of vampire lore, of course."

As Sophie walks with Heather to officially place *Harry Potter and the Sorcerer's Stone* in the adult fiction section, she stops and looks back at Jacob.

"Have you really read all of the Harry Potter books, sir?" she asks.

"Twice," he says. "And when my wife is finished, I'm going to read them again."

The little girl beams at him, clutches the book to her chest, and bounds down the aisle.

9

"Banned Books Week"

"Late September is a special time for booksellers," Julia explains to Sal and Camden as she unpacks the promotional materials they received for this year's Banned Books Week. "We get to celebrate freedom of speech while pissing off a number of people in the process. Your uncle loved it."

"Banned Books Week," Sal repeats. "I've heard about it, but never paid much attention."

"That's ironic," Camden replies, "given that you spent most of your life doing banned things."

"Cute," he says. "So please explain what Banned Books Week entails, Julia. Given all the stuff you've got there it looks like a lot of work."

"Well, it does take some work, but it's so much fun," she says. "It almost never gets any media coverage, but book censorship of all kinds, including book burning, continues right up to today. Anyone who's offended by just about anything in a book can and will challenge it: parents, teachers, clergy members, elected officials, organizations, you name it."

"What do you mean by challenge it?" Camden asks.

"I mean try to keep out of schools and public libraries," she answers. "Raise enough stink, and council members and school administrators sometimes take the easy way out and cave in to the demands of the few."

"But what reasons do they give for not wanting the books to be available?" Camden asks, having a hard time making sense of it.

"They usually object to what they consider inappropriate language, violence, sexual or racial themes, or religious viewpoint," Julia answers.

"I thought America was founded on freedom of speech," Camden muses.

"Sometimes the ones who speak the loudest determine who has the freedom," Sal says. "What does the store usually do for the week?"

"We set up a display of books that have been banned in the past—you'll be surprised by a lot of them—do readings, stuff like that. As much as anything, it's about the freedom to read and educating people on how fragile that freedom can be if we don't protect it. The libraries will all have events as well."

"Sounds fun," Sal says. "We get to be bad, call attention to the fact we're being bad, and maybe even make some money at the same time. My kind of week."

A week later Banned Books Week is in full swing. Julia has jumped into the event with both feet and is giving a mini-lecture to a group of customers who are looking over some books that have been placed under a large "Can You Believe These Were Banned?" sign.

"As you can see," she says, "a number of the books on this table are considered classics by most people. Yet some, both when they were published and even today, think they are simply too controversial for you to be trusted with them. For example, fundamentalist religious groups have been challenging the Harry Potter books since the first one came out in 1997."

Several of the customers shake their heads in amazement. The titles are indeed some of the best-known and best-loved works of literature ever published. They range from *The Adventures of Huckleberry Finn* to *The Great Gatsby*, from *To Kill a Mockingbird* to *Gone with the Wind*. Arranged with them are more recent examples like *The Perks of Being a Wallflower*, *The Kite Runner*, and *The Golden Compass*.

"Independent bookstores," Julia continues, "have traditionally taken the lead in supporting freedom of expression, from City Lights Books' Lawrence Ferlinghetti publishing Alan Ginsberg's *Howl*, to Shakespeare and

Company's Sylvia Beach publishing James Joyce's *Ulysses*. Both books were initially banned, yet the bookstore owners were not intimidated. In Mr. Ferlinghetti's case, the result was a Supreme Court ruling that established a legal precedent for the publication of controversial work with redeeming social importance."

Sal walks up to the group, catching the end of her presentation.

"You can all help support independent bookstores, and defend the Constitution," he says, "by buying some of these books. Heck, buy them all; we'll order more."

There is scattered laughter, some of it uncomfortable, but several of the customers do indeed pick up some of the books and take them to the counter.

"Great presentation, Jules," he says. "Just remember to ask for the sale at the end." At that moment, Camden hurries up to him.

"Please go rescue those poor people from Heather," she says. "She is ranting about the number of Hemingway's books that have been challenged or banned at various times."

Sal walks over to where Heather has a small group cornered, but does not intervene immediately. He expects the sheer entertainment value of her rant to be quite high.

"*The Sun Also Rises, A Farewell to Arms, For Whom the Bell Tolls*...all banned or challenged at some point. This was a man who won a Pulitzer and the Nobel Prize!" She is definitely getting worked up.

"Hemingway won the Nobel Peace Prize?" a man in the group asks.

Heather turns on him in a flash, and he takes a quick step back. She regains her composure before speaking again.

"No, sir," she says through clenched teeth. "He won the Noble Prize for Literature in 1954."

"Oh," the man replies.

"And here's something I found extremely interesting," she says, returning to her subject. "*A Farewell To Arms* was threatened with removal from high schools in the Dallas Independent School District in 1974, forty-one years after it was burned in the Nazi bonfires that attempted to destroy every book Hitler found offensive."

"Are you comparing Dallas to Nazi Germany?" asks the same idiot who asked about the Nobel Peace Prize. Some people don't know when to be quiet. Heather wheels on him again.

"I'm not comparing anything," she says with a sneer. "I think everyone here is smart enough to draw their own logical conclusions. I'll just say that Fascism didn't disappear in 1945."

The man seems, foolishly Sal thinks, to want to say more. Before he can, Sal grabs a handsome young man standing nearby and thrusts a copy of the aforementioned *A Farewell to Arms* into his hands.

"Let's just see what Hitler was so scared of," Sal says. "Sir, would you please read the first page of Chapter One for us?"

The young man seems slightly embarrassed, but reluctantly complies. As Sal hoped, as soon as Hemingway's words about Italy at the time of World War I begin to roll from the man's lips Heather's expression changes. She relaxes visibly, and after a few paragraphs begins to look longingly at him as he reads. After what he considers a long enough interval, Sal stops him.

"Thanks so much," he says. "Great job. In fact, you can keep the book, no charge." He hustles the young man, the Nobel idiot, and the rest of the group to another part of the store. He returns shortly to check on Heather. She still has a faraway look in her eyes.

"You okay, kiddo?" he asks.

"Great," she answers, "though not as great as I'd be if I could have dragged that guy you made read into the back room for a while."

"Sorry," he says. "I realize it was reading interruptus, but it was all I could think of to prevent possible bloodshed."

"I understand," she says with a sly smile. "So, want to go to the back room for a while?"

"I don't think that would be such a good idea," he says.

"I think you're afraid it would be a very good idea."

"That too," he agrees. "How about we step outside for a smoke instead?"

"I guess that will have to do for now," she says. "But it could have been such fun."

"Isn't it pretty to think so?" he replies with smile.

10

"Fifty Ways to Love Your Lever"

Sal comes downstairs late and hung over. He expects to find the store filled with people; instead he finds only the staff. It is a full forty minutes past opening time, and the sign on the door is still turned to "Closed."

He can see a large group of customers through the glass; one looks at her watch and leaves. Sal surveys the store; everyone, it seems, is reading, and reading the same book. Even Jacob is engrossed, oblivious to the time or the customers outside, one of whom has begun rapping on the glass with a car key.

"What the hell is going on here?" Sal shouts across the store, shattering the dead silence that had previously been broken only by the slight rustle of pages turning.

Everyone looks up simultaneously, and if he didn't know better, Sal would have thought by their expressions they were little kids caught doing something they shouldn't. Julia stares at him with a look of horror, turns a deep crimson, then puts down the book (reluctantly, it seems) and rushes to unlock the front door. Heather begins straightening one of the fiction shelves. Camden slides the book into her purse, while Siren Two simply goes back to reading. Sal walks up to Jacob and starts to speak, but Jacob tosses him the book before he can.

"See for yourself," he says as he moves slowly toward the Rare Books section. "It'll grab your attention, but it sure isn't literature."

Sal looks at the book. The cover is black with simple white lettering: *The Forbidden Fruit* by A. C. Whitman.

"No relation to Walt, I assume," Sal says under his breath.

He doesn't recognize the title, and knows he didn't order any copies, let alone the two stacks by the checkout counter. A table by the front door is also filled with copies.

"I didn't order this," he says to Julia.

Even as he says it, he notices three women already in line to pay; all have copies of *The Forbidden Fruit*. One has three copies.

"I ordered it," Camden replies as she comes up behind him. "This book is going to save our month, and maybe our year. Every woman in town is going to want it."

The three women at the counter, Julia, and the Siren all nod in agreement.

Later that afternoon Sal and Camden are eating lunch at a deli near the Tarrant County Courthouse. It is past 2 p.m., and the lunch-hour crowd has thinned. A copy of the book sits on the table between them.

"It's pornography," Sal says between bites of a pastrami on rye. "I will not sell this trash in my store."

"*Our* store," Camden corrects him. "It's actually classified as erotica. And when did you become such a Puritan? You were the one who enjoyed Banned Books Week so much. I suppose now you're going to tell me that misunderstanding with someone's mother was over china patterns."

"I'm no Puritan," he replies, "but this is smut. If you want this kind of stuff you should get it where everyone else does...the Internet."

"You mean where every *man* does. What's online does not cater to a female clientele. This book does, and it's not that poorly written."

"Not poorly written?" Sal says, actually putting down his sandwich now. "It makes Dan Brown and Stephenie Meyer look like Faulkner and Steinbeck. And I only read the first 30 pages."

"Well, I suppose you are a better judge of literary quality," she admits. "But I know what sells. And this baby will sell."

Sal looks at her in astonishment.

"Did you just say 'this baby will sell'?" he asks. "What happened to my proper English cousin?"

"She has a store to run and mouths to feed...well, one mouth anyway. I would think you of all people would be on board. Imagine, a gangster put off by a couple of sex scenes. What would Lucky Luciano think?"

"You leave Lucky Luciano out of this," he says sharply while making the sign of the cross. "God rest his soul. And it's not a couple sex scenes. The sex scene started on page one and never stopped as far as I could tell. And how did you even find it? I've never even heard of it."

She pauses to take a drink of her tea and hesitates before answering. He drums his fingers on top of the book.

"A friend from England told me about it a while back. It was originally self-published in London by a well-known dominatrix and—"

"Wait," he says, interrupting her. "A well-known dominatrix? You have dominatrixes, or whatever the hell the plural is, over there that are well-known? Like celebrities?"

"The English are not as uptight about sex as you Americans are," she answered.

"You're obviously not English then," he says, "or at least you weren't until you brought this abomination into my shop."

"*OUR* shop!" she screams across the table, causing heads to turn. "And it is not an abomination for crying out loud; it's a book."

"Whatever," Sal replies, then attacks the pastrami on rye again. It is a poor imitation of what the serve back home; the food is the thing he misses most about Jersey. "Did you see how embarrassed Julia was when I caught her reading it? You're even corrupting Jacob."

"His wife was in earlier...bought a copy for herself and one for each of her sisters in Arizona."

Sal groans and starts to light a cigarette.

"What is it with you and smoking in public places?" she asks. "You can't smoke in here, you dolt."

"Why not? This area's not zoned for adult bookstores either, but apparently I'm running one anyway."

He puts the cigarette back in the pack and pushes his empty plate away.

"So finish telling me how you found this peppy little tome," he says.

"Like I said," she continues, "it was self-published, but word of mouth brought it to a publisher's attention. It's not even officially out in the States yet."

"Not even online?" Sal asks. "Everything's available on Blue Nile."

"The author detests Blue Nile and won't let them carry it," Camden says. "She's very much about buying from

High Street shops; over here you call it the 'Buy Local' movement. She even hates shopping at Tesco."

"Tesco?"

"The British version of Wal-Mart."

"I thought Wal-Mart was the British version of Wal-Mart," Sal says.

"Arrogant American," Cam says. "Anyway, she's very local business oriented. I've heard all her leather comes from a craftsman in Cardiff, Wales."

"Nice," Sal says. "But even if it's not online, surely the big-box retailers here are selling it."

"Not one of them," she says, shaking her head. "It's quite salacious, as you've seen, and the big chains are afraid to carry it because of the chance of protests."

"Protests?"

"Yes," she says with a hint of satisfaction. "By the Episcopals."

"I think you mean the evangelicals."

"Right, them. I got our copies from the British distributor, then put word out to a few key people, and we have a run that hasn't stopped since we opened."

"Forty minutes late."

"Yes, forty minutes late, so shoot me."

"Don't tempt me, your grace. So if we're getting them from the UK, we're paying overseas freight. Where's the profit?"

"Well," she says, "we got a good discount because of how many I ordered and half off shipping. Since the price is in pounds, Julia and Heather and I just slapped on a price sticker in dollars that has no correlation to the exchange rate. They're paying whatever we ask."

"Smart. Wait, you said a good discount? How many did you order?"

"Five thousand copies," she says, beaming.

"Five *thousand* copies? Are you insane? At the sticker price, even with a discount of 40 percent—"

"45 percent," she says proudly.

"That still comes out to…" Sal stops in midsentence, furiously trying to do the math in his head.

"$32,750.00," Camden says calmly. "Plus shipping."

Sal looks at her for a long while, then looks down, rubs his eyes, gets up and walks out of the deli muttering to himself.

"Camden Templeton sleeps with the fishes."

Back at the shop the scene is pure chaos. They have had to bring in an extra Siren just to help keep some semblance of order inside. Sal can't even get through the front door; he can only look through the front windows and watch *The Forbidden Fruit* fly off the shelves.

He steps away from the shop and notices Jacob sitting on a bench across the street. Sal crosses the street and sits down next to him.

"Not reading the book, I see," Sal says.

"Nope," Jacob replies. "I prefer Steinbeck and Tolstoy to that kind of nonsense. Just wanted to see what the fuss was about. If you want something blue, rent a tape."

"Using the terms 'blue' and 'tape' put you a couple decades behind the times."

"For God's sake boy, I run the Rare Book room. Of course I'm behind the times." He pauses for a moment, and then continues. "I just wish I knew what your uncle would have done in this situation."

"He'd have never sold that trash," Sal said.

"Maybe, and maybe not." Jacob absentmindedly strokes his beard. "He loved literature, which makes me say no. But he liked keeping the place going, so maybe yes. Given his proclivities with the ladies right up to the very end, I think the tiebreaker goes to yes."

"Then where do we draw the line, Jacob?"

"That's one only you and your cousin can answer," Jacob says, getting up from the bench. "You two run the place now, remember?"

Jacob crosses the street headed back to the shop. As he reaches the door, Julia exits. She sees Sal, crosses the street, and takes a seat next to him.

"I just had to get out of there for a minute," she says. "It's been nuts all day. And please ask Camden to order another 1,000 copies with rush delivery. I think tomorrow may be worse."

Sal shakes his head and lights another cigarette.

"Can I bum one of those?" Julia asks. "I usually only smoke when I drink, but it looks so good right now."

Sal fishes a cigarette out of the pack, gives it to her, and lights it.

"I feel like I'm contributing to the delinquency of a minor," he says.

"But I'm *not* a minor," she replies with a wink, then inhales deeply.

"I suppose that's true," he says, then catches himself looking at her for a moment too long and changes the subject. "What do you think about us selling this book, as someone with a degree in Literature, I mean?"

"I see the pros and cons," she answers. "Obviously the writing is crap, but most porn actors can't act, and no one cares about that."

Sal laughs and nods in agreement.

"And it's hard to turn down the amount we can make with the book selling like it is," she continues. "Plus, it is an actual book they have to read. Besides, I'm using the subject matter to our advantage."

"How exactly are you doing that?" he asks, suspicious.

"I put stacks of *Wuthering Heights* and *Madame Bovary* by the register. Whenever someone buys *The Forbidden Fruit* I tell them they should check out how this stuff was put out for women in the 18th and 19th centuries. Been selling a ton of both. I ordered extras when Camden told me about *The Forbidden Fruit* coming in."

"Jules, my dear," he says, "you are a genius."

"Nice of you to notice."

"I still don't think my uncle would approve of us selling a crap book, even if it does make a ton of money."

"It is poorly written," she agrees, "but Mr. Templeton would probably have loved a lot of the scenes. You saw some of the…items…in his room, right?"

He is momentarily at a loss for words.

"I have seen the items," he answers. "But I'm surprised you have."

Her eyes widen and she answers quickly.

"I never saw them personally," she stammers. "But the Sirens talk. A lot."

Sal gives her a smile and pats her knee, which causes her to flush a deeper red.

"That's good to know," he says. "There are some things that should not be kept in the family."

He stands, takes her hand and kisses it lightly, then walks back toward the store. She is sitting in the exact same spot, a smile on her face, when he stops and looks back. He turns around and walks up to her again.

"Say, would you be at all interested in seeing what I did not take from that safe in Ithaca that I was nowhere near that night?"

She nods vigorously.

"Great. We could grab something to eat first. We can leave after we close the shop."

A smile spreads across her face, which causes Sal to smile as well.

"Are you asking me out on a date, Mr. Terranova?"

"Why, yes I am, Ms. Hall. Is that a problem?

"Not at all," she says, still smiling. "But we shouldn't leave together. The Sirens will talk."

"Really?"

"Definitely."

He considers this for a moment. He hadn't really thought through the implications of them working together when he made his rash offer, and he certainly did not want either of them to have issues with the rest of the staff.

"Okay," he says. "Meet me at Billy McGee's at 9:30."

The rush has thinned somewhat by early evening; the legions of women who eagerly snapped up *The Forbidden Fruit* having apparently rushed home to begin devouring the book. Sal is enjoying the lull when a man frantically sprints to the counter.

"Do you sell hammers?" the man spits out.

"Say again," Sal says, certain he heard the man wrong.

"I need to buy a hammer," the man repeats, even more flustered than before.

"This is a bookstore," Sal says in a voice he would use when explaining things to a small child. "We don't sell hammers."

"Neither does anyone else on this block, and I need a hammer!" The man looks like he might cry.

Sal actually does have a hammer upstairs that he would gladly sell the man, but he decides to have a little fun instead.

"Exactly why do you need a hammer so bad?" he asks.

"My cat is missing," the man explains hastily. "I need to post these flyers." He holds up a sheaf of papers; the top one shows a full-color picture of a cat wearing an argyle sweater. The cat does not look amused.

"And that requires a hammer because…?"

"So I can nail these up around the neighborhood. I tried tape but the wind blew them all off."

"I see. Well, maybe we have something you could use instead." He leads the man to a shelf of books. "A Bible is heavy enough, but the nail would punch through the leather, and there's the possibility of angering the Almighty, which is never good."

The man nods in agreement. Sal suddenly understands why the cat ran away. He walks over to some mystery paperbacks and picks one up.

"Not nearly heavy enough," Sal says. He finally stops in front of a display stacked high with copies of *The Forbidden Fruit*. He picks one up, studying its mass. "Heavy enough," he says to the man. "Hardcover, no redeeming literary merit. Perfect." He hands the book to the man, who starts to protest.

"Twenty percent off," Sal tells him. "Our cat lover's discount."

The man considers this, nods, pays, and rushes out of the store. As Sal leans back down over the morning's sports page, Heather walks over to him.

"Did you just sell a copy of *The Forbidden Fruit* for use as a hammer?" she asks.

"I did indeed," he answers without looking up.

"Awesome," she replies.

11

"A Lucky Discovery"

Billy McGee's is little more than a bar and glorified hamburger joint, but its location downtown makes it an upscale dive. Its signature feature used to be the peanut shells everyone threw on the floor, but that ended when a drunk woman in six-inch heels slipped on a shell and sued them. Still, it was a lively place with 80s music on the sound system and really cold beer.

Sal and Julia are seated at a booth near the back of the restaurant. Julia is not wearing her glasses, and her hair falls loosely around her shoulders. Her eyes appear darker without the glasses, and Sal recalls his initial thought upon meeting her the first time. She is a stunner.

There is a bucket with four beer bottles on ice on the table; two more are open in front of them. There are also several pounds of unpeeled, boiled shrimp spread out across butcher paper between them. They are peeling the shrimp and throwing the peels into a second, empty metal bucket.

"I'm impressed," Sal says.

"At what?"

"You peel your own shrimp. A lot of women would have given me a disgusted look and a ration of crap for even suggesting it."

She smiles and dunks her just-peeled shrimp into a dish of cocktail sauce. She then grabs some French fries from a basket and dunks them too.

"So, you promised to show me what the super-secret thing is that you didn't steal while you weren't in Ithaca."

"Patience, my dear, patience. Shouldn't we act like normal people and have some grown-up conversation first?"

"Can you do either?"

"Either?"

"Act either normal or grown-up?"

He gives her a hard look, but she does not react. He looks harder. Nothing. Then she bursts out laughing.

"I'm just messing with you. Your inability to act like a normal person is part of your charm. And the fact that, maturity-wise at least, I'm actually older than you makes our real age difference not such a big deal."

"Thanks...I think. So, what are the chances that this S&M book my cousin is peddling will lead to repeat customers? Unless we're selling whips or handcuffs, they have no real reason to come back."

"They'll be back," she says, "some of them at least. Remember, before this crazy day most of them had no idea we even existed. Now they do. I also told everyone that came in about the book clubs we're starting on Tuesday and Thursday nights. More than twenty people have already signed up online."

"Book clubs...what a great idea. Why didn't I...wait, did you say they signed up online?"

"Yeah," she says, dunking another shrimp.

"We have a website? Since when?"

"Since the day the computers were delivered. Camden asked me to set it up."

"Huh. Somehow I missed that too."

"My job is to not miss that kind of thing," she says. "One of many reasons you need to keep me around." She smiles sweetly, peels a shrimp, and holds it up for him to take a bite. He does.

"Julia, are you flirting with me?"

"I am, and I'm doing a far better job of it than you are. I thought mobsters were supposed to be suave."

"You've been watching too many Scorsese movies. Most of us are really shy wallflowers."

"Right," she says with a laugh. "That describes you perfectly. So, you realize the rest of the staff already thinks we've got something going, right?"

"What? Why do they think that?"

She pats his hand and opens two more beers.

"You really are adorable, even if you are the boss. For starters, I suppose they've noticed we're never more than a few steps from each other whenever we're both in the shop."

Sal ponders this for a moment.

"I think you're right. You really need to stop following me around like a lovesick teenager. It's not professional."

With one flick she bounces a shrimp off his head. It ricochets off the window, bounces once on the table, and then lands in her water glass.

"I'm the one who's unprofessional?" she replies. "You're always late—"

"I don't do mornings well."

"...you teach Ramon how to pick locks—"

"It's a useful skill."

"...you harass poor Jacob constantly—"

"He likes the attention."

"...and worst of all, you shamelessly flirt with the Sirens and any other woman under 80 who walks in the store."

"Just good public relations," he says, arching an eyebrow. "Why is that the worst of all?"

She doesn't answer immediately, playing with a French fry and not looking at him.

"It just bothers me, that's all. Anyway, enough banter. You lured me out tonight with the promise of secrets being revealed. Show me the fruits of your infamous alleged heist."

"Can't. It's back at the apartment."

Her smile fades, replaced by a look of disappointment.

"But Camden will be there."

"So what? If everyone already thinks we've got something going, then—"

"Absolutely not."

Sal laughs and holds up his hands in mock surrender.

"Relax, Julia. It's fine. Cam's going to a midnight screening of *The Rocky Horror Picture Show* with Heather, with whom she has oddly bonded. And in costume, I think. Apparently she did this all the time back home...who knew? Sadly though, she will be home at some point, so no sleepover for you tonight."

"I guess I'll just have to go home and pine away for you then."

"Of course, if you don't have a roommate..."

"Nice try. And that was almost suave. Almost. Let's finish this shrimp; the suspense is killing me."

The apartment has changed drastically since the first night he and Camden saw it. The furniture is new, and from the décor and general tidiness, it is obvious a woman lives here. Julia looks around, impressed.

"I know it looks like a chick's apartment," he says, "but I can assure you my room is pure man cave. In fact, it may be too man cave for you to see at the moment. It's the maid's month off."

"I have three older brothers; nothing will shock me."

"Okay, but you've been warned," he replies, opening the door and stepping aside for her to enter.

Julia looks around the room. It is very large, more the size of a den than a bedroom. A nearly floor-to-ceiling window looks out over the alley behind the shop. The bed is pushed into the far corner. There is a recliner positioned in front of a large flat-screen TV and a desk with a chair on one wall.

Bookcases line the remaining walls. Unlike the bookcases in the hall and living room, these contain books, lots of them. The walls, except for the one with the window, each have a single adornment: a huge framed poster from Springsteen's *Born in the USA* tour, a framed poster from the film *The Usual Suspects*, and a giant, green New York Jets flag.

"Well, the place certainly has...character."

"Have a seat," he says, pointing to the recliner.

She sits, and he walks over to one of the bookcases. He reaches up to the top shelf and pulls down an old leather journal. He slides the chair from the desk so he is facing her, then he hands her the journal.

"What's this?" she asks.

"The fruits of my infamous alleged heist."

She turns the book over in her hands, then opens the front cover and reads the first page aloud: "*Our Thing*, by Salvatore Lucania. Dannemora, New York, May 1937." She gives him a questioning look, then her eyes widen.

"Oh my God!" she exclaims.

"What? What's wrong?"

"Salvatore Lucania was Lucky Luciano's birth name. This is his journal from when he was in prison!"

"How in the world did you know that was Lucky's real name?" he asks, amazed.

"I saw a show about him on Crime TV," she says, as if the answer should be obvious. "It was actually on the same night as the one about you, strangely enough. They moved him to the prison in Dannemora to get him out of New York City."

"Right. Wow, you are full of surprises."

"Not as many as you. How did you get his journal?"

"Uh, sweetie, I stole it, remember? Even though I was really in Hoboken."

"Atlantic City," she says with an exasperated sigh. "Good lord, why can you never remember your own alibi? I'm afraid you may fold under questioning, Sal."

"Cute," he says. "And it's not his journal. It's a novel."

"A novel? The founder of organized crime in America wrote a novel?"

"Yep. It's not great, mind you, but it's better than *The Forbidden Fruit*. And the gangsters are the good guys."

"Of course they are. Why have I never heard of it before?"

"It's not something that's common knowledge. More of an urban Italian legend. Since there's only the one copy, even most mob guys don't believe it ever really existed."

"But it does," she says. "Or does it? Are you sure it's real?"

"Handwriting's legit. The age, paper, everything matches. I've searched for this thing since I was 8 years old."

"You're kidding. Since you were 8?"

"No lie. I loved books and I loved Charlie Luciano. I wanted to be him when I grew up. So when my dad told me the story of the book, I started looking for it."

She hands the journal back to him. He caresses the cover before putting it gently back on the shelf.

"How did you find out where it was?"

"It's a long story, really long. The short answer is John Gotti."

"*The* John Gotti?"

"The very one. He went after that thing like Hitler went after the Ark of the Covenant. Well, I had an uncle in the Gambino Family who was close to John, and by following what he told me about Gotti's search I narrowed it down to five possible people who could have it. I got lucky on number four, no pun intended."

"But none of the news reports said anything about a book being taken from the safe, especially not one that would be as big a deal as this."

"The guy never reported it stolen. He had most likely either had it stolen or bought it hot himself. You tend to stay quiet about things like that."

"Is that all that was in the safe?"

"Nah, there was lots of stuff. A fair amount of cash, some loose diamonds, and a shitload of German bearer bonds, like the dude was Hans Gruber from *Die Hard* or something."

"So no one knows about the book?"

"Just me and the guy I took it from. He can't be positive it was me, of course, and couldn't do much even if he was. I gave the bonds to my Capo back home, and he kicked some up to the Boss. The diamonds went to the Boss over the territory that includes Ithaca, to keep the peace… I was a long way from home on that job. I kept the cash and the book. Everybody assumes it was a huge score, which it was. But not the way they're thinking."

"Any idea what the book would be worth, like at an auction?"

"Conservatively, around $400,000, maybe more. Maybe much more to someone who's really into that kind of thing."

Julia is not sure she heard him correctly.

"Did you say four hundred *thousand* dollars?"

"Yeah."

"And you have it just sitting on a shelf?"

"It's hiding in plain sight. No one knows it really exists, so no one's looking for it, at least now that Gotti's dead."

"Shouldn't you put it in a safe deposit box or something?"

"Sweetheart, a guy like me renting a safe deposit box at a bank arouses a lot of attention."

"Right; I didn't think about that. And I guess you can't just take it to an auction house. So are you trying to line up a buyer, discreetly?"

Sal shakes his head, and his expression changes.

"Darlin', I will never, ever sell this book. It's a piece of history I've spent my whole life chasing, and most of the time I didn't even know for sure if it was real. I'll die penniless before I ever sell this. If my mother needed the money for a heart transplant, and the only way to get it was to sell this book...I'd miss her. I wouldn't sell it for four hundred million dollars. Never. Ever."

"Well, at least you don't have irrationally strong feelings about it. What does Camden think about something this rare just sitting on a shelf in your apartment?"

"Cam doesn't know," he says. "Like I said, no one knows. Just me, probably the guy in Ithaca, and now you. And it's gonna stay that way."

Her eyes start to fill with tears. Alarmed, he jumps up.

"What? Why are you crying? What did I do?"

"You told your deepest secret to *me*," she says, wiping away some tears. "On our first date. Now that is suave."

She stands up, puts her arms around his neck, and kisses him. It is a long, slow kiss. Then she steps back.

"I hate to say this, but I should probably go before Camden gets back."

Sal looks at his watch. The movie is certainly over by now.

"Damn it! I guess so. I didn't realize it had gotten so late. I'll walk you home."

"It's only four blocks, all through well-lit, touristy, and heavily patrolled Sundance Square. I'll be fine."

"It would be ungentlemanly of me to let you go into the night alone."

"With the number of cops down here every night keeping the out-of-towners safe, you're in more danger than I am."

"For you, kiddo, I'll take that chance."

He locks up the apartment and they walk out into the street. It is a clear, pleasant night, with stars and a quarter moon visible. After a few steps, Julia slides her hand in his.

12

"The Midway"

Sal is on his way out of the store one evening when Jacob stops him. He is running late and doesn't want to hear Jacob rattle on about how the Russian authors don't get enough respect, but then he sees that there is a customer with him. He is a tall, lean man roughly the same age as Jacob, with a mop of unkempt white hair and a regal bearing. Sal hasn't met many people with a regal bearing.

"Sal," he says. "I'd like you to meet Charles Moriarty."

Sal shakes the man's hand; he has a firm grip.

"Please accept my belated condolences on the passing of your uncle," Charles Moriarty says. "He was a great bookman, and one of my best friends for half a century."

"Thank you, sir," Sal says. "He was one of a kind."

"Charles owns Moriarty & Son's Booksellers," Jacob says. "It's about an hour from here, near Hillsboro."

"Please come visit us some time," Mr. Moriarty says. "I'd love to show you my little shop, and tell you some stories about your uncle that would certainly amuse you."

"I'd like that," Sal says.

"Well, I had better be going," Charles says. "It's a long drive back home. Good to see you again, Jacob, and thanks for the book. My customer will be thrilled that we found the Dostoyevsky so quickly."

He shakes Sal's hand again, nods at Jacob, and is gone. Sal is even later now, but can't leave without asking Jacob about this man. Camden walks over after finishing with some customers.

"Who was that man, Jacob?" she asks. "You were a lot friendlier with him than you are most customers."

"That was a friend of Uncle Franklin's," Sal says. "He owns a bookstore too."

"Not just any, son," Jacob says. "A very special bookstore."

"What's so special about it?" Camden asks, intrigued.

Jacob takes a drink from his coffee mug before answering, pleased to have their full attention. He settles back on his stool behind the counter.

"His bookstore is special for many reasons," he says, "most of which can't be explained but rather have to be seen. We should take a trip down there one day."

They both nod, and Sal glances at his watch again.

"What I can tell you is this," he continues. "You have both marveled at the fact that this store has been open for more than 50 years. Well, Moriarty & Sons has been a fixture in their city ever since Trevor Moriarty arrived following the destruction of his Galveston bookshop in the Great Hurricane of 1900."

"That was the storm that destroyed the whole city of Galveston, right?" Camden asks. "That one even made the history books in England. We do love our tales of woe."

"The very same," Jacob says. "That Trevor arrived at all was a miracle in itself; he and his family were vacationing in Denver when the storm struck. The store and all of its contents were lost; more tragically, three employees perished on that terrible day.

"The newly relocated store thrived from the day the doors first opened. Trevor later became the first book dealer in the state to extend his business nationwide through the use of mail order sales. When he died in 1947, or maybe it was 1948, his son, James, took over the shop; it passed to James's son, Charles, when James retired in the early 1970s. Charles runs it now, and he's still holding out hope that his son will take over from him."

"So the bookshop has been open for over 100 years, in different locations," Sal says admiringly.

"Not even close, Sal," Jacob says. "Before Galveston they were in Savannah, Georgia, and by that time they had already been in existence 200 years. You can trace Moriarty & Sons Booksellers from here back through Galveston,

Savannah, and London all the way to Manchester, where the first Moriarty opened their first shop in 1602. Four hundred years of continuous ownership."

"Four hundred years?" Camden exclaims. "You mean it's possible that one of my ancestors bought a book in their shop in London 300 years ago?"

"Definitely possible," Jacob says. "There's a lot you two could learn just by listening to that gentleman's stories. He's forgotten more about books and bookselling than the three of us combined will ever know."

Sal looks at his watch one last time: he is most definitely late.

"We'll make plans to visit his store," he says as he heads for the door. "Right now I am very late, and my date will not be happy."

The night is clear and pleasantly cool. Sal and Julia walk through the travelling carnival that has arisen overnight in the parking lot of Rangers Ballpark in Arlington, home of the Major League Baseball team. The team is on a road trip to the west coast to finish out the season, and the stadium owners have seized the opportunity to make some money with their otherwise empty parking area.

Lights flash, music blares and rides thunder. Pre-school aged children squeal with terror and delight on the mini-rollercoaster with cars the shape of a long Chinese dragon, older kids munch popcorn and cotton candy as their parents wolf down giant corn dogs and turkey legs, and teen boys try to win huge stuffed animals for their dates. It is a controlled chaos, and Sal loves it. It isn't Coney Island, where his dad took him a few times as a kid, or even Asbury Park, but it will have to do.

"I have to warn you," Sal says. "The Midway is a dangerous place for me,"

"Really?" she asks. "Why is that?"

"I have a weakness for carnival games," he answers. "And the inability to resist carnies."

"Oh no," she gasps in mock horror. "Should we escape while we can?"

"No. I'll try to remain strong."

There was actually very little chance of Sal remaining strong. Some people have a weakness for alcohol or drugs or food or sex. Sal's great weakness was the Midway...and the carnies. The carnival games beckoned to him from the moment he entered an amusement part, the State Fair, even a church fall festival. It was odd, because he rarely gambled on horses or cards or sports, so it wasn't a gambling weakness. It was a carny weakness. They called out to him and he followed, like the snakes following St. Patrick out of Ireland.

The night starts out well enough. They watch some little kids ride goats twice their size, eat corn dogs, and ride a few rides. On the Chamber of Horrors ride Julia snuggles up to him the entire time, even though the chamber contains no actual horrors and not much that is even mildly scary. He tells her about meeting Mr. Moriarty, whom she had actually met several times before; she had even visited his store once. Then, as they are walking to the Ferris wheel for a view of Arlington at night, disaster strikes.

"Hey there," says a deep, raspy voice, "win a prize for the pretty lady."

Sal should have just kept walking. He knew what would happen if he turned to the carny, but just like the girl in the horror movie always opens the door she knows she shouldn't, he always heeded the call of a carny. To walk past, to admit defeat at the outset, was something his pride would simply not allow. He stops and turns.

As soon as he sees the carny, the game and the prize, he knows he is screwed. The game is one of his least favorites, one where you have to toss two softballs into a peach basket and both have to stay in the basket for you to win. It is such a rigged game they don't even bother with the escalating prize system where you drop a ton of cash by winning small prizes that have to be traded up for bigger ones, like trading venial sins for mortal ones. The peach basket/softball scam has only one giant prize, but it is nearly impossible to win (like shooting the entire red star out of the target with a BB machine gun) while seeming like it should be simple, so you just keep dropping more and more money. The prize at this booth is an enormous purple gorilla, and Sal can see immediately that Julia loves it.

Throughout history, men of all ages have done far dumber things to impress a girl, but few have had the deck as stacked against them as Sal does this night. Not only is the game nearly impossible to win, the carny is impossible to resist, even more than normal carnival folk. That is because, in what can only be the universe blatantly mocking Sal, this bearded beanpole has not one, but *two* lazy eyes. Every time he speaks they spin around crazily, completely independent of each other, like someone is turning separate cranks inside his skull. When those eyes spin and he says "c'mon, give it one more try for the little lady," Sal is helpless.

The game sounds easy, as all Midway games do. One peach basket with a large hump in the bottom set at roughly a 45-degree angle at the back of the booth, two softballs, and a giant gorilla. Get both balls to stay inside the basket and win the gorilla. Problem is, the first ball always stays in the basket while the second always bounces out like it has been shot out of a cannon. Sal's theory has always been that before the second throw the carny engages a spring of some sort in the humped part of the basket that is wound tight enough to launch a shuttle into orbit. It sounds crazy, but...

The cost of the game is $2.00 for 2 softballs, which is cheap enough. If he can spend just a few dollars to get the big monkey, then no problem.

The first ball nestles softly in the basket, causing that moment of exhilaration one always feels on the verge of winning. The second ball bounces back so hard it flies over his head. Julia laughs; he slaps down two more dollars. Again the first ball settles gently into the bottom of the

135

basket. He tosses the second even more lightly; it shoots straight up in the air and hits one of the purple gorillas.

When he is ten dollars down, Julia suggests they just walk away.

"I don't have anywhere to put a giant purple gorilla in my place," she says halfheartedly.

"Don't give up now, my boy," the carny goads, spinning one eye while rolling the other up and down.

"Two more balls," Sal says.

The ensuing series of throws go this way: in the basket, over his head, in the basket, over the top of the booth, in the basket, into the forehead of a bystander who leans in too close.

At twenty dollars down, a crowd has gathered around the booth; some encourage him, others stare at the carny's eyes. Julia has stopped protesting, drawn in by the same lazy-eyed hypnosis that has gripped Sal.

"You're getting close, son," the carny assures him. "I can feel it."

He slaps two bills down on the narrow railing.

"Two more balls." One ball in...one not.

At fifty dollars down it seems that all other activity on the Midway has ceased, suspended in the ether as Sal wages war with this diabolical peach basket and, by extension, this demonic carny. Everything has disappeared from his consciousness: the crowd, the noise, even Julia. As the second ball skitters out of the basket for the twenty-fifth time, Julia puts her hand on Sal's cheek, forcing him to look at her.

"If you are trying to impress me," she says sweetly, trying to break the carny's hypnotic grip with a hypnosis of her own, "you did that twenty dollars ago. Now you're starting to freak me out a little."

Sal ignores her plea and pulls the remaining cash from his pocket: three crumpled one-dollar bills and enough ride tickets for the Ferris wheel and the Tilt-A-Whirl. He also holds his jacket back just far enough for the carny to see his gun.

"I've got enough for one more try," he tells the carny. "And what time did you say you got off work, friend?"

Julia shakes her head, then kisses him on the cheek. She cannot see the gun from where she stands.

"Go ahead," she says, and steps back so she won't be injured when the second ball inevitably rockets out of the basket. "Try not to put your eye out," she adds, then flushes crimson as she looks at the carny's eyes.

But the carny's expression has changed, and amazingly his eyes have stopped moving. He has turned white as a sheet.

"On a date, huh?" asks the carny in a higher-pitched voice than before. He watches Sal with one eye and Julia with the other, then nods gravely at Sal. "I feel really good about this time. You're due."

Sal hands the man two dollars and throws the first ball, which remains lodged in the basket as always. Before he can throw the second, the carny stops him.

"That one's scuffed," he says. "Use this one."

The ball he hands Sal must weigh three times more than the others. Sal looks at him and the carny nods, his expression sheepish and conspiratorial at the same time. He throws the heavy ball; it lands in the basket with a loud thud, cracks two of the wooden slats, and stops dead.

The carny breathes a sigh of relief and grabs a long pole to retrieve one of the purple gorillas from its hook. Julia throws her arms around Sal's neck and kisses him, long and soft. The crowd behind him erupts with joy and relief, then quickly disperses. Julia takes the gorilla from the carny and Sal shakes his hand.

"Keep it honest," Sal says, trying to look into both eyes at once.

"Right," says the carny. "And if you don't mind me saying, maybe you should consider avoiding the Midway from now on. It seems to make you a little nuts."

Julia nods in agreement and leads Sal away from the booth. They walk hand in hand to the Ferris wheel, Julia clutching a purple ape almost as big as she is. They decide to skip the Tilt-A-Whirl and ride the Ferris wheel twice. When they see the lights of the city from the top of the wheel, they know it was the right call. Even the ape seems to agree.

13

"The Education of Salvatore Terranova"

The morning started out gray and windy, with the promise of storms later in the afternoon, but the weather doesn't dampen Sal's mood. He is beginning to love seeing life from the inside of a bookstore, and this morning is about to become one to remember.

The front door opens and the wind carries in a light mist along with a woman, who in turn is carrying a box that can only contain books she hopes to sell. She is an elderly lady, probably around seventy years old, petite with closely cropped gray hair. Sal might have called her frail had she not handled what was obviously a heavy load with such apparent ease. He hurries around the counter and takes the box from her.

"If you're looking to sell these, ma'am, you may have to wait until our used and rare buyer gets here; he's due in at noon."

"Really?" she says, breathing easier after he takes the box. "I'm not sure I can wait that long. I'd really like to sell these, but no one seems to want them. They belonged to my husband; he passed a few weeks ago."

"I'm sorry," Sal says. It's what you are supposed to say, but he knows it never gives anyone much comfort.

"Thank you," she says. "He's in a better place now. I'm Claudia Jones."

She extends her hand and Sal shakes it, careful not to squeeze too hard.

"Sal Terranova," he says. "Why doesn't anyone want them?"

"I suppose because they're old library books," she replies. "Everywhere I've called said they don't have any use for them. I only came down here because I've bought romance novels from Mr. Templeton." She blushes slightly and lowers her voice. "I know it's scandalous for a woman my age, but I still like the romances and the trashier the better."

Sal laughs out loud; he is beginning to like this little lady, and briefly considers recommending *The Forbidden Fruit* to her. But he also knows he won't be able to do any more than the other stores she contacted. There simply is no market for ex-library books, even in perfect condition. He ponders the idea of just giving her a couple bucks a book for her trouble, then he opens the box and looks down at what might be a winning lottery ticket. He opens the top book and realizes it is better than that.

"Julia!" he shouts toward the back room. "Call Jacob and tell him to get up here now."

When Jacob arrives, grumbling about unreasonable bosses, they all gather at the counter. Sal introduces Mrs. Jones, explains the situation, then pulls out the book that was sitting on top. He carefully hands it to Jacob, whose eyes widen. Jacob opens it to the copyright page.

"First edition, first printing," Sal says. "And it's signed." Jacob is momentarily speechless, but Sal is not.

"Mrs. Jones, what made you think these were library books?" he asks.

"Walter—that was my husband—liked going to library book sales, and these have the plastic cover like library books, so I just assumed. Are they not?"

"No, ma'am, they're not," Jacob answers. "These are clear plastic archival covers. They protect the dust jacket from damage, and people only use them for first editions and other books they think are, or will be, valuable."

"Do you mean these are valuable?" she asks, her eyes wide with surprise. "I almost dropped them off at Goodwill just to get rid of them."

"We'd have to look at each one," Sal says. "But I can tell you this one is valuable because it's one I've been wanting for years."

He holds up the book to show her. She still doesn't seem to believe they aren't ordinary former library books.

"This is a first edition, first printing, signed copy of John Dunning's *Booked to Die*. It's something of a legend in the book collecting world because it's about an ex-cop in Denver who opens a rare bookshop. When it first came out in 1992, there were only 6500 copies printed. The first run of a book is called the first printing, or first impression, of the first edition. A book may only have one printing, or it may have five, or even fifty for a book like *The Da Vinci Code*.

"However, collectors always want that first printing, and with only 6500 copies out there, it was bound to become valuable if the book had any success at all, which it did. This one is also signed and dated in the year of publication, which makes it even more valuable. A reputable dealer will usually offer you between 25% and 40% of the retail value. That's standard because you never know how long it will take to sell, and they have the overhead costs in the meantime."

Jacob has taken a step back and is watching Sal interact with this lady. He nods approvingly.

"I had Jacob come in to look at these because he's the expert," Sal continues. "He can tell you what all your books are worth in a fraction of the time it would take me. As for this book, I want it for myself, not the store, and I'll offer you full price right now."

Jacob stops smiling and jabs Sal in the ribs.

"You don't have that kind of money," he whispers.

"I've got a little stashed away for a rainy day," he answers. "I'll never see another one of these again."

"What would full price be?" Claudia asks.

"Let's look," Jacob says. "These things can fluctuate, and it's been a while since I last saw what this one was selling for."

Sal pulls a chair up to the counter so Mrs. Jones can see the computer Jacob is using to look up prices. He shows her multiple sites, each with a range of prices. He finally determines a fair offer and whispers it in Sal's ear. Sal doesn't hesitate.

"I can give you $1,200," he says. "Cash."

Claudia Jones seems as if she might faint. She looks from Sal to Jacob then back to Sal.

"$1,200 for one book," she says. It isn't a question so much as a statement of astonishment. "$1,200 for a book I was going to give to Goodwill."

"Yes, ma'am," Sal says. "And you've still got a whole box we haven't gone through yet."

"A box?" she replies. "I've got a whole room full at home. These are just the first ones I grabbed."

Sal looks at Jacob, who now looks as if *he* might faint.

"You mean you have an entire collection like this?" he asks.

"I sure do," Mrs. Jones answers. "Would you like to come see it after we're done with these?"

This time Sal hesitates; Jacob doesn't.

"Julia, please watch the shop," he yells across the store. "Sal and I are going to go make this lady an offer on some books."

Claudia sits in a straight-back chair in her late husband's study while Sal and Jacob try to take in the scope of his book collection. The box she had brought into the store had held, in addition to the Dunning book that Sal bought, fifteen more books of varying value, including signed first editions of Stephen King's first four books. All told, paying her 40% netted Mrs. Jones $5,130 plus the $1,200 Sal had given her.

She still didn't seem to believe that this was happening to her, but the check from the store and the cash from Sal were real enough, and she was content to watch the proceedings from her chair. The quality and diversity was amazing: everything from the latest Janet Evanovich to *The Sun Also Rises,* all first editions. The Evanovich was signed and would retail for around $35; the Hemingway was unsigned and would go for at least $11,000. Sal would have to keep this one away from Heather; the temptation to steal it might prove too great for her, and the shop already had one criminal.

At one point Sal called Camden and told her to pull all the cash she could find (including a fat envelope taped to the underside of one of his dresser drawers) and deposit it in the store's account. She refused until Jacob took the phone and told her the amount of profit they could make when he sold the books, which he was sure he could do quickly. In the end, Camden relented; a discovery like this came around once in a lifetime.

It turned out that Mrs. Jones was selling just about everything and moving to San Diego to live with her younger sister. Jacob asked if there were any children or grandchildren she might have wanted to give some of the books to, which was a difficult question but one that in good conscience had to be asked.

"One daughter and a couple of grandkids who never have time to come around," she says bitterly. "I won't be leaving anything for them."

When they finish they give Mrs. Jones an itemized breakdown of each of the books, with expected retail and what the payment would be to her. She had the option of taking the offer as a whole, removing some of the books, or rejecting them outright if she wanted a second appraisal by another dealer.

"Nonsense," she says. "You folks have been wonderful to me when you easily could have paid me next to nothing; I'd have never known the difference. I'll take the offer, and be very happy about it."

I'd be happy too, Sal thought. From what she once thought were old library books, Mrs. Jones would make a handsome sum: around $20,000 for everything, including the first box and the book Sal bought for himself. Not a bad nest egg for Mrs. Jones to take to San Diego, and some great stock for the store.

After loading the last boxes, Sal and Jacob wish Mrs. Jones well and thank her for giving them the opportunity to buy such fine books. They will ultimately go to collectors, which probably would have made her husband happy.

"That reminds me of something," she says. "Just give me one minute."

She hurries back into the house, and while she's gone Jacob looks at Sal and smiles.

"Good day, huh?" Sal asks.

"In more ways than one," Jacob answers. "We got some great books, and you impressed me."

Before Sal can ask what the hell that means, Claudia Jones returns holding a large leather journal. She hands it to him.

"Walter kept a diary of all the time he spent looking for books," she says, then hesitates. "No, he wouldn't call it a diary, that's a girl thing. What would he call it?"

"A journal?" Sal suggests.

"Yes, a journal. Anyway, he kept a journal with notes on most of the books he bought, at least until he got sick. It probably tells how he got that one book you like so much. I want you to have it."

She hands the journal to Sal. It is, he sees now, very thick, and bound with genuine leather. It almost looks like a Bible.

"It was like his own personal Bible," she says, as if reading his thoughts.

"I can't take this, ma'am," he says, although he really does want to. "This seems like a personal thing you'd want to keep."

"What's so personal about a bunch of notes on books? I've got more than forty-five years of letters, cards, notes, photos, and home movies. I won't miss that book, and I think you'll appreciate it."

He would indeed. Sal could learn a huge amount just by reading the way this man went about collecting books. And he needed all the knowledge he could get. It was a tremendous gift, worth more than even the copy of *Booked to Die*.

"Thank you, Mrs. Jones," he says. "I'll take good care of it."

"I know you will," she says with a smile. "That's why I gave it to you."

Back at the store, they finish unloading the books and then go outside for some air. The expected thunderstorms have not arrived yet, but still threaten. Sal pulls a cigarette out of his pack, and noticing him eyeing the pack, offers one to Jacob. Jacob hesitates, then takes it.

"I don't smoke much anymore, but after a morning like this I just want one," he says as Sal lights it for him.

"I know," Sal says. "I've seen you sneak one after a really good purchase before."

"Okay," Jacob says after taking a deep drag from the cigarette, "what did you learn today?"

"Well, I didn't have a lot of time to learn anything before Mrs. Jones came in," he replies.

"Everything you learned came *after* Mrs. Jones came in. Give it some thought."

Sal wracks his brain…*what had he learned?*

"Well, I learned that something amazing can come through the door when you least expect it."

"That's one, for sure," Jacob replies. "And you have to be on the lookout for those rare times or you'll miss them. You could have done the same thing the other places she called did: told her that used library books have no resale value and not even looked at them."

"But they weren't library books."

"And you were smart enough to recognize that. Knowledge really is power in this business. What else?"

"I don't know…always be fair to the customers?" he ventures.

"Always be *honest*. You could have taken that whole box for 20 bucks and no one but you would have ever known. But you didn't. You did the right thing, which is why I said you impressed me earlier. Given your history, I didn't expect it."

"I was tempted, I have to admit. It would have been nice to get that Dunning at a cut-rate price."

"That's a different lesson, one you need to improve on," Jacob says. "There was no reason for you to pay full price for that book. You could have paid the 40% just like on all the others and the lady would still have been thrilled, but you let your desire for the book and feeling sorry for her cloud your judgment. Now there's no way you can make a profit on it if you decide to sell it."

"I'm not selling that one," Sal protests.

"I get that," he replies, nodding and tossing the cigarette butt into a cylindrical container at the same time. "I probably wouldn't either. But it's a fine line between collector and seller. You can't fall in love with the books...they're your livelihood. Not commodities in the conventional sense, but at the same time that is exactly what they are. And on a buy like the one today, you usually can't afford to keep even one for your collection. Keep one, and you end up keeping more, and pretty soon you're working at a car wash."

"I'm still keeping the Dunning," Sal says with a smile, but a little defensively.

"And you should. But the rest get sold. Very soon, if we're lucky."

As it turns out, they sell several that same day, including the four early Stephen King novels. Jacob is also certain he can get a good price on five signed Tom Clancy novels from a dealer in Baton Rouge. It appears they might actually turn a profit on the buy before the end of the month—and on books that were actually good, not just porn-on-paper. Jacob would be insufferable about it, but for Sal that's a fair trade.

14

"Camden and the Book Scout"

It is early on a quiet Wednesday morning, and it is a good thing it's quiet because the bookstore is seriously understaffed. Jacob has called in sick with a very bad-sounding cough; it is especially worrisome given his age. Heather is having car trouble, Siren One has jury duty, and Sal is nowhere to be found.

The front door chime rings and Camden looks up to see a man in his late 20s, not quite scruffy but not well scrubbed either, carrying a large box. She has seen him in the store a few times before, but has never spoken to him. He moves quickly to the counter where Jacob evaluates books people bring in to sell and sets the box down with obvious relief. Camden walks to the counter.

"Good morning," she says. "Can I help you?"

"Yes, ma'am," the man replies. "I've got a load of books for Mr. W. to check out."

She ignores his calling her ma'am (they are too close in age for that), gives the man her best apologetic expression, and shakes her head slowly.

"I'm sorry, but Jacob is out sick today. Hopefully he'll be back tomorrow. Could you bring them back then?"

The man makes no move to pick up his box. He just smiles at her.

"Is there anyone else who could make me an offer on them?" he asks.

"Sal could—he's my cousin and partner—but he isn't here either."

"Ramon?" he asks. "I know Mr. W. has been teaching him the ropes."

"No," she says, "he won't be in until 4, after he gets out of school, and he's not authorized to make purchases yet anyway. Has Julia ever made offers on books?"

The man laughs and shakes his head.

"I'd love to have her buy them," he says, "but Jacob would kill me, or worse, never buy from me again. Julia loves old books, and her sentimental streak causes her to offer far too much for them. Great for me, but bad for your business."

Camden nods; she can see how this could be true.

"I have an idea," the man continues. "Why don't I show you how Jacob would determine a price on these?"

Camden eyes him warily, then shakes her head.

"I don't think so, Mr...."

"Scott," he says. "Not Mr. anything, just Scott." He holds out his hand and she shakes it.

"Nice to meet you, Not Mr. Anything, Just Scott. I'm Camden. And I'm afraid you might fleece us worse with me pricing these than if I let Julia do it."

"No fleecing allowed," he says. "I promise. I'll even show you the ways Mr. W. looks up the current values. In exchange for this invaluable instruction, you can either give me 5% more than the price he normally would, or you can have coffee with me later and I will regale you with intriguing tales of book scouting."

Camden feels her cheeks flush; it has been a while since anyone flirted with her, even if it is a scruffy guy trying to get a better payout for a box of books.

"I don't know," she says. "I'm not sure I can take the time right now. We're awfully busy."

Scott looks around the store; there is not a single customer. He turns back to her and arches an eyebrow. She looks around as well, then laughs.

"Fine," she says. "I'll indulge this exercise for a moment. What would we need to do?"

"It's a simple process," he replies, "which doesn't mean it's always easy. Jacob and I argue over his valuations about half the time. For the purposes of our mini-class today, I'll argue with myself."

Camden laughs again, finding herself being taken in by the man's humorous charm. If he was the one Julia had been buying from, maybe it wasn't her sentimentality about books that caused her to pay more than she should.

Scott unpacks all of the books and lays them out across the counter. Then he walks around to her side of the counter.

"It's easier if we're on the same side."

She is wondering if he intended the double meaning she read in the statement when a loud bellow comes from the front door.

"Get back on your side of the counter, Scott!" Jacob yells.

Jacob looks like death on two legs, and Camden is afraid the effort it took to yell might have been too much for him. He shuffles slowly to the counter and leans against it, breathing heavily. He glares at both Camden and Scott.

"I'm gone one morning..." he says, the sentence broken off by a coughing fit.

"Jacob," Cam says, "what are you doing here? You can't even stand."

"I'll be fine," he says, recovering his voice. "My wife was driving me crazy anyway, and I can sit while I plow through the substandard books this guy has brought in."

His words are harsh, but his tone is playful, a combination Camden has never heard before. It appears

Jacob has a soft spot for this scruffy book scout. Which reminds her of something.

"What is a book scout, anyway?" she asks.

"A book scout," Scott says, "is a rare soul who makes his living through the discovery, acquisition, and sale of rare and collectible volumes. We are literary treasure hunters, bibliophilic adventurers, men not content to be trapped in the conventional prison of office and time clock. We are, sadly, a dying breed."

"In other words," Jacob translates, "a scrounger who can't hold down a real job."

"That too," Scott agrees with a crooked smile.

"Sounds interesting," Camden says. "Where do you find the books?

"Anywhere and everywhere," Scott says. "Thrift stores, rummage sales, auctions, dusty attics."

"Why don't you take her down to Abram Street and show her how it's done?" Jacob asks.

"That's a good idea," Scott agrees. "Nothing like a little hands-on experience. Every bookseller should know how to scout for books."

"As enticing as that sounds," Camden says, "we're short on staff today."

She has barely finished the sentence when Heather and Siren One both walk into the store. They head straight for her.

"Car's fixed," Heather says. "It was just a loose battery cable."

"And I didn't get picked for the jury," Siren One says. "Apparently asking if the death penalty is an option for an alleged drug dealer upsets the defense attorney."

They both walk to the checkout counter, and Scott turns to Camden.

"You were saying?"

"I was saying...that I do not know you nearly well enough to just go off scouting for books with you by myself."

"I'll go with you," says Sal, who has suddenly materialized behind her. "Heck, I'll drive. I love looking for books."

"Where have you been all morning?" Camden asks, wheeling around to face him.

"The Pancake House," he says. "It's Free Pancake Day, and the line was really long."

She stares at him as if he is a backward child, wondering if he can possibly be serious.

"You can't be serious," she says.

"Sure I can," he says. "They have great pancakes. Let's go find some books."

Thirty minutes later Sal is driving the three of them down Abram Street in East Arlington. He is fairly familiar with the area; he drove around here one night after getting lost following a Yankees/Rangers baseball game and returned several times because it reminded him of parts of Newark. There is a general feeling of decay to the place, with its auto body shops, thrift stores, and *taquerias*. It is the thrift stores they are here to see.

The first stop is the Dal-Worth Resale Barn, which is not housed in a barn but rather in run-down building that had once housed (according to the sign that still stands out front) a Winn-Dixie grocery store. There is a blind man selling pencils near the front door; he is not wearing pants.

"You have got to be kidding," Camden says, taking in the neighborhood, the building, and the pantsless blind man.

"Nope," Scott assures her. "This place can be a gold mine if you hit it at the right time."

"How is that even possible?"

"Easy," he says. "This is a very old neighborhood, as you can see. In fact, I grew up here myself."

"Really?"

"East side all the way," he says. "Anyway, more than a decade ago, probably longer, young Hispanic families starting moving here for the schools and to get out of Oak Cliff and West Dallas. As happens in these situations, it caused the younger white folks to flee west, leaving only the older folks who had lived their whole lives here and wouldn't or couldn't leave."

"Fascinating as this bit of demographic trivia is," she says, "I don't see what it has to do with finding books in this dump."

"Let me finish," he says. He turns to Sal. "Is she always this impatient?"

"Yeah," Sal says, "always."

"As I was saying," Scott continues, "there ended up being a high percentage of older people. Those older people came from a generation that enjoyed reading books rather than playing on computers, and those older people also started dying since they were, well, old."

"I see where this is going," Sal says. "Let me try to fill in the rest. Granddad dies, and among the many things he has packed into his house over the decades is a bunch of books. The kids or grandkids are tasked with cleaning everything out so the house can be sold or rented, and they have no clue what to do with shelf after shelf of books, especially since they probably have none in their own homes. It's easier to just donate them than to have a yard sale, so they drop the whole lot here, or one of the other places along Abram Street."

"Very good," Scott says. "And while most of it is crap—encyclopedias, Readers Digest Condensed Books, Time-Life series stuff—sometimes the book gods smile down on you. It's not always something scarce that Jacob snaps up; sometimes it's just a really nice copy of a common title that you pay a quarter for and sell for two bucks. Though even that is harder to do now than it used to be."

Before Camden can ask why it's harder now, Sal and Scott have entered the store and made a beeline for the books. She hurries to catch up, not wanting to be left alone in an establishment that allows people with no trousers to sell pencils on their property.

The store's book section is quite large; there is no debating that. It is also the most jumbled mess she has ever seen. Forget alphabetization; there aren't even sections separating fiction from non-fiction. Books are piled on the floor, and some are still in boxes. The charity shops of London would never allow such slipshod merchandising.

Sal and Scott have both taken a seat on the floor, which Camden doubts has been mopped since the place was a grocery store, and are pawing through the bottom shelves.

"Always start with the lowest shelves, Camden," Scott tells her. "Most people are too lazy to get all the way down here to look properly. I find my best stuff on the bottom."

"What's the best book you ever found?" Sal asks him.

"Price-wise, you mean?" Scott asks.

"Yeah, or just your favorite."

"Best one-book profit I ever made was on a signed first edition of Perez Reverte's *The Club Dumas*," he says. "Found it at Larry McMurtry's store in Archer City. They have so many books there that they never get around to re-pricing them as values go up; I paid thirty dollars for it and sold it to Jacob the next day for $250. It's probably still in your store."

"Nice," Sal replies. "What about your favorite?"

"That one I found at a Friends of the Library sale," he says proudly. "A signed first of Dan Jenkins' *Semi-Tough*. Not super valuable—you can get one online for $75.00— but I love Jenkins, and he didn't sign a lot of his books. An old woman was punching me in the kidneys trying to get at some Danielle Steele paperbacks, and as I turned to retaliate I saw it."

"So what exactly are we looking for?" Camden asks, still refusing to join them on the floor.

"First and foremost," Scott says, "condition, condition, condition. A book in poor shape isn't worth squat, no matter how collectible it might be otherwise. You always want the first printing of the book, and if it's signed that's even better."

"Sal's explained first printings and points to me," she says. "Are all first printings valuable?"

"I wish. Most aren't worth anything as far as resale. But sometimes even a bad book can be worth a ton if you have the first printing."

"Even a bad book?" she asks.

"Yes," he says. "For example, *The Da Vinci Code* will never be mistaken for great literature, right?"

"Hardly," she says with a derisive snort.

"But it sold more than 60 million copies in *hardcover*, which is unheard of unless your name is J.K. Rowling. More than 99% of the copies you find, like those three over there—" he points to the third shelf of a nearby case, "—are worth about a dollar, there are so many of them. But if you find a first printing the price jumps to $500, and if it's signed it can go up to $1,000 or more. In this case you're collecting both the scarcity and the hype."

"Okay," she says. "Anything else I should watch for?"

"The dust jacket has to be perfect," Sal tells her. "Crazy as it sounds, up to 90% of the value of a book comes from the dust jacket."

"Very true," Scott says. "And I also look for books that came out before the 1980s, before they started putting barcodes on them."

"Why is that?" Sal asks. Camden is pleased to see he doesn't know everything. She is also glad he asked because she cannot fathom how a barcode could reduce a book's value.

"Remember me saying earlier that it's hard to sell common books now?" They both nod. "The main reason is that everyone and their brother sells books online now. And they all have apps on their phones that allow them to scan the barcode of a book and immediately find out its current value. But they're lazy, like the people who ignore the bottom shelf; they go right past a book with no barcode, which leaves a lot of good stuff just waiting to be found."

On the way back to the shop that afternoon, having hit multiple stores and found nothing at all, Camden is thinking about the online booksellers Scott mentioned.

"I've been wondering if we should sell books online," she says. "Do people sell a lot that way?"

"A lot of books get sold that way," he says, "but very few make any money at it. Between the auctions sites, personal websites, and Blue Nile the prices are driven down to the point that it's break-even at best. Blue Nile is the only one that really makes anything selling books online, and only because they've driven so many stores out of business."

"Bastards," is Sal's only comment.

"So you don't sell online yourself?" she asks him.

"Nope. I'm an analog guy in a digital world."

"I wish we all still were," Sal says.

When they arrive back at the store, Camden goes straight upstairs to clean up after her adventure in the thrift stores. Sal and Scott walk to where Jacob had been pricing Scott's books when they left. Jacob is dozing on his stool behind the counter, but he leaps up when Sal says his name, which immediately sends him into another coughing fit. Sal and Scott rush over to him, but he waves them away.

"I'm fine," he manages to say between spasms. "Where have you been?"

"You know where we've been," Sal says. "You sent us there."

"But I needed to talk to you."

"You could have called my cell phone," he answers.

"Or even mine," Scott adds.

"No, no, no," Jacob insists. "This must be done face to face."

"What?" Sal asks. "You resigning or something?"

Jacob frowns, then coughs more, which does not prevent Sal from laughing.

"No, I'm not resigning," he says. "Though I should. You'd all be lost without me."

"Right," Sal says. "Just ships adrift."

"Mock me all you want, boy, but I found one of your uncle's missing books. What do you have to say about that?"

Sal stops laughing.

"What? Where?"

"Right here," Jacob says, tapping his index finger on the top book of a stack in front of him. "It was in the box Scott brought this morning."

Sal picks up the book and examines it. It is Trollope's *The Way We Live Now*, not the original 1875 edition, but rather a very beautiful edition put out by the Folio Society of London in 1992. As Jacob had said earlier, it is not particularly expensive, maybe $125 retail, but it is a fine volume. And there on the front free endpaper is the Franklin's bookplate. Sal turns to Scott, who is accepting a small stack of bills from Jacob for the books.

"Where did you get this book?" Sal asks earnestly.

Scott takes the book from him and looks hard at it.

"Ah," he says, remembering, "I got it at an estate sale about a month ago. Guy didn't have a great collection, but there were a few good ones. This was one of them."

"Do you have any idea where he got it?"

"It was an estate sale, Sal," he says. "The guy was already dead."

"Oh, right." He thinks for a minute. "Any heirs we can ask?"

"I don't believe so. If I recall correctly he had no family left; his wife had died a few years ago. Sorry."

"That's okay," Sal says, his shoulders slumping a little. "At least we found this one. And now I know the books are out there somewhere. I just have to find them."

"I'll be glad to keep an eye out for you," Scott says. "I don't know how I missed the bookplate in this one; it's not like me. What else can you do to locate them?"

"I don't know," Sal says. "I'm not even sure where I would start. But I'll think of something."

"I can put the word out to a few guys I know," Scott says. "The more eyes the better."

"Thanks," Sal says, shaking his hand. "It's not much, but it's a start."

15

"You Say You Want a Revolution"

Just after the store opens on Friday morning, Ramon walks through the front door. Sal looks up from a box of books he's sorting through, surprised.

"No school today, sport?" he asks. *Or are you cutting class again?*

Ramon has a downcast look, like someone just ran over his dog.

"No school for me at all anymore," he replies. "I just got expelled."

There are gasps and stunned looks from all of the staff and even a few customers. Camden rushes over to him.

"Expelled?!" she half asks, half shouts. "Why?"

"Has to be drugs," Jacob says as he walks to the front of the store.

"Guns," says Julia.

"Sleeping with the Home Ec teacher," says Sal. Heather and Siren One smile and nod, but Ramon shakes his head.

"None of the above," Ramon says. "Apparently the principal didn't like my manifesto."

Sal and Camden exchange glances, and Julia hangs her head.

"Your what?" Heather asks, confused.

"My manifesto. I published a very rough draft in the school paper. Uncle Luis and I aren't finished with it yet, but I wanted to get some feedback, some kind of reaction."

"Looks like you did," says Jacob. Julia jabs him in the side with a pencil. Ramon nods.

"Yeah, I guess so. Mr. Throckmorton decided it was terroristic in nature and kicked me out. 'Zero tolerance,' he said. I should have left out the part about J.A.F.T."

"J.A.F.T.?" Sal asks.

"The troika that will govern when my people rise up and throw off their shackles. I call it the Junta Against Free Thought – J.A.F.T."

Jacob walks away shaking his head and muttering: "Commies...right here in Fort Worth."

"But what about your right to free speech?" Camden asks.

The others turn and look at her like she's from another planet, or worse, England.

"You're about a decade behind the curve, ma'am," Julia says. "Kids have no rights in schools now."

"What did your mother say?" she asks, patting him on the shoulder. Now *he* looks at her like she's from another planet, or worse, England.

"I'm not telling my mother," he says, horrified at the thought. "Esmerelda Ines Maria Ortiz-Sanchez does not have children who get expelled. My only hope of living to my next birthday is to join the Marines and then send her a letter explaining things – from Afghanistan."

"The Corps would straighten you out, that's for sure," Jacob says, having just returned to the group.

"And the uniforms are pretty," Julia adds.

"Let me make a phone call," Sal says. "By tomorrow your principal will be in a 55-gallon drum at the bottom of the Gulf of Mexico."

Ramon's expression brightens, but Camden shoots Sal a withering glare.

"Let's not go to the mattresses just yet, Clemenza," she says to Sal.

"Of course not, your ladyship," he replies. "I suppose you're going to go over there first and charm this principal into submission with your logic, charm, and accent." He says 'accent' quite sarcastically.

"That is precisely what I'm going to do," Cam says.

Ramon appears unconvinced; the drum-at-the-bottom-of-the-Gulf seems like a much better idea.

"I need to make a quick call," he says, reaching for his cell phone. "I can take you to the school after lunch." He dials a number and walks out the front door.

That afternoon, Camden and Ramon are seated in front of Principal Throckmorton's desk, in chairs likely designed to provide as little comfort as possible. Camden wears her most professional suit, something she has not done since she left London even though her mum had shipped all of them to her along with her other belongings. Ramon wears his usual attire: jeans, T-shirt, and Doc Martens.

Throckmorton sits in a high-backed leather chair on the other side of the desk. He is a small, balding, almost effeminate man in his late 50s. His look is impassive, though slightly sympathetic.

"Tell me again, Ms. Templeton, what is your relationship to Ramon?"

"I'm something of an advocate for him in this matter," Camden says.

"In an official capacity?"

She hesitates, not having expected to be questioned herself. She shifts uncomfortably in her chair, feeling like she's the one back in school standing before the headmaster.

"Well, I'm not a barrister or anything like that, but we have a professional relationship."

"I see," he says. He forms a tent with his hands and stares hard at them. He clearly does not see. "In any case, while Ramon may indeed be one of the brightest seniors here at Ben Milam High School, we simply cannot condone or ignore this sort of inflammatory rhetoric. He was inciting violence."

"Inflammatory rhetoric?" Camden repeats. "It was an editorial in a school newspaper, not a sermon on al-Jazeera."

Throckmorton starts to reply when the door to his office swings open; the light from the outer office is completely blocked by the form of a huge man filling the doorway. Before entering he leans back into the outer office and speaks to the secretary.

"Nine o'clock tomorrow night at The Blarney Stone will be perfect, my dear."

He closes the door, walks to the desk, and shakes a clearly flustered Throckmorton's hand. He then kisses Camden's hand and nods at Ramon. He does not sit.

"I am Luis Ortiz," he says. "I am young Ramon's uncle, benefactor, and mentor, the Socrates to his Plato, the St. Paul to his Timothy, the—"

"Vito to his Michael?" Camden interjects.

Luis turns to her and flashes a brilliant smile, clearly pleased.

"I was going to say the Fidel to his Che," he says, "but yours is much better."

Camden flushes at the compliment. Ortiz is truly a compelling figure, well over six feet tall and at least 250 pounds with not a bit of fat evident. He has light blue eyes that sparkle when he speaks, and his voice is melodious though his English is heavily accented. The slight gray at the temples of his short black hair puts his age at roughly 40, but he has the unlined face of someone ten years younger.

Throckmorton starts to speak, but Ortiz raises his hand, cutting him off.

"My nephew is high spirited and intellectually curious," he continues. "Traits surely nurtured under your expert tutelage. Perhaps his article went too far in some respects, but he is obviously not expelled. A week of detention will suffice, though even that is unwarranted. Let us go, Ramon."

Ramon stands, but Camden remains seated, as dumbstruck as the principal, who still has not gotten a word in. Throckmorton leaps into the brief pause.

"I don't care who you are," he says, "or what you said to my soon-to-be ex-secretary to gain entrance to my office, but the boy is indeed expelled."

Ortiz turns back to the principal, sighs, motions for Ramon to sit, then walks to the window. He opens it and glances outside.

"This is a grand old building," he says. "Built in 1937, if I am not mistaken. You can tell by the fact that it has windows that open; new schools have no windows at all. Beautiful architecturally, but quite unfortunate for you." He steps away from the window.

"Unfortunate for me? What are you talking about?"

Camden gasps as a small red dot appears on the principal's forehead. He gives her a questioning look, unaware of what is happening. She points to his forehead.

"A dot," she says excitedly. "On your forehead."

He still doesn't grasp what's going on until the dot slides down to his coffee mug, where he can see it, then up his arm and back to his head.

"You really must alter your decision in the next thirty seconds," Ortiz says calmly. "My comrade Jake has to preach a revival in Dallas in 45 minutes, so he cannot observe you through his rifle scope indefinitely."

With surprising agility, Throckmorton dives under his desk. Ortiz smiles and makes a gesture out the window. The red dot disappears. He then leans down and looks at Throckmorton, who is wedged as far under his desk as humanly possible.

"Be a man," Ortiz chides him. "Besides, you have to come out sometime. Eventually you must go home to 4137 Aspen Court, or perhaps to your sister's house at 312 10th Avenue. Even as far as your mother's home in Tulsa, though I do hate to involve people's mothers in unpleasantries. Do we have an understanding?"

"I'll...I'll...call the police," he stammers in a high-pitched squeal.

"Oh my!" Luis exclaims. "The police! You have so terrified me that I may have soiled myself a bit."

In spite of herself, Camden laughs at this. Luis looks over and winks, then leans down again.

"*Mira*," he says to the cowering form under the desk. "Someday my nephew will run this country, or some other country nearby. He can do that without a high school diploma, but he should not have to, and therefore will not have to. So again, do we have an understanding?"

Throckmorton stammers from under the desk.

"How...how do I know that wasn't just a regular laser pointer from an office supply sto—"

Before he can finish, Ortiz motions at the window then quickly steps between Camden and the far wall, shielding her. The glass covering a framed diploma from Oklahoma State on Throckmorton's wall suddenly explodes into a shower of fragments, and a large hole is visible in the center. Camden is wide-eyed, but does not scream. Ramon simply smiles. Ortiz moves back to Throckmorton's hiding place and leans down.

"You were saying?"

"Yes, yes! The boy is reinstated!"

"Excellent! I do hope your successor is as prudent."

"My successor?" he asks, still not moving from under the desk.

"You made me ask twice, made my dear friend late for church, and upset this lovely lady. You will, of course, have to resign."

"What? I'm not resigning."

Ortiz looks at his nephew.

"Ramon," he says, "at the gym today I ran like a god, but was unable to use the weights due to my pressing appointment here. Perhaps I should pick up this large oak desk and drop it on our hesitant administrator a few times instead."

"Perhaps, Uncle."

"No, please, no! I'll do whatever you tell me."

"Ah," says Luis. "Excellent. Let us go, Ramon, and lovely lady friend of Ramon."

They walk out of the office, leaving Throckmorton under the desk.

"Hello?" he calls after they have walked out. "Can someone help me? I seem to be stuck under here."

That night after the shop has closed, Sal, Camden, Julia, Ramon, and Ortiz sit at a table at the Blarney Stone, eating Irish nachos and drinking beer, except Ramon, who drinks tea. The Blarney Stone is a bar and grill styled after a New

York pub, with live music and an outside patio. Sal feels right at home.

The Blarney Stone is strategically placed just off the UT – Arlington campus. When it first opened decades ago, James Donovan decorated the place himself, and since there weren't a huge number of Irish celebrities in his era, he had covered the walls with pictures of John Wayne, various New York Yankees, and lots and lots of Italians. They include Frank Sinatra, Dean Martin, Sophia Loren, Joe DiMaggio, Jake LaMotta, Rocky Marciano, Lucky Luciano, and Pope John XXIII. There is also, much to Sal's delight, a picture of Bruce Springsteen, even though The Boss is only half-Italian. A portrait of Bono hangs over the front door, the only Irishman in evidence.

The wall behind the stage is covered with a huge Irish flag, and a sign over the front door reads "No Dogs or Englishmen Allowed." Camden took offense at this when they first walked in, but Luis had easily calmed her. A large jar on the bar solicited donations for the poor starving children of Belfast, but anyone with any brains knew every dime went to the IRA. In the late 1970s and early 1980s, the Cause had been fashionable with college kids, and donations during that period were plentiful. No doubt those poor starving children were furnished with more than a few pipe bombs and AK-47s.

The tables are serviceable, if a little worn, but the main bar is a thing of beauty. Carved from solid walnut, it gleams as if someone polishes it every hour. Arranged neatly on shelves above the back bar, in front of the wall-length mirror, are bottles of every kind of liquor known to man; the only country with no bottle represented is England, for obvious reasons.

"So," Ortiz says, "The Professor is running a bookstore. Quite unexpected."

"As unexpected," Sal replies, "as *la Vibora* working for a preacher...sniper...which is he?"

"I'm a bit of both," says a voice behind him.

A large, solidly built man about the same height as Ortiz but thirty pounds lighter steps into view. Ortiz leaps up from the table.

"Jake, my brother!" he exclaims, enveloping the man in a bear hug. "I am so sorry for making you late for your soul-saving event."

"No worries, Lou," he says. "I assume the principal ultimately saw things your way."

"Indeed. But I am forgetting my duties as host." He gestures to everyone at the table. "Jake, these are my new friends, Camden, Julia, and Sal. Everyone, this is Jake Donovan."

Handshakes and greetings are exchanged, and Jake takes a seat at the table with them. He and Ortiz both down a shot of tequila. Jake calls for a round for the table, except, of course, for Ramon. A man with a striking resemblance to Jake brings over a tray, passes shot glasses around, and takes one for himself.

"On the house," he says after he throws back the shot. "Sally Fingers doesn't pay for anything in my bar." He slaps Sal on the back and walks away.

"Who was that?" Sal asks, caught off guard.

"That," Jake says, "is my brother, Eddie. He runs the place."

"And you're James Donovan's son?" Sal asks.

"Indeed he is," says Ortiz. "And my best friend since I was eighteen."

"Who is James Donovan?" Camden asks.

"He was the head of the mob in this town for years," Julia tells her. As soon as the words leave her mouth she looks at Jake, horrified. "I am so sorry...I didn't..."

"It's okay," he says. "Pop was what he was."

Ortiz smiles and pats Julia's hand.

"I am happy the younger generation knows their history," he says.

Relieved, Julia smiles. Camden is looking around, taking the place in, when she realizes something.

"No one is dancing," she says to no one in particular. There is a band playing, and they are very good, yet not a single person is dancing. There doesn't even appear to be a dance floor. "Why isn't anyone dancing?"

"Much like dogs and Englishmen—no offense—dancing is sadly not allowed," Ortiz says.

Even Sal is taken aback by this. He looks from Ortiz to Jake, wondering if they're joking. Jake reads his thought.

"It's no joke," he says. "We're within one thousand feet of the First Baptist Church, and a city ordinance passed in 1897 says we're too close to allow dancing. We can serve alcohol, but no dancing."

"That is the most ludicrous thing I've ever heard," Camden says.

"Welcome to Texas," Julia says. Then she thinks of something herself and turns to Sal. "Luis called you The Professor," she points out. "But Eddie called you Sally Fingers. Can you have more than one street name?"

"I don't have a street name, angel. That's for criminals."

"What about Ithaca?" Ortiz asks.

"I was in Asbury Park that night."

"Atlantic City," she corrects.

"Right. Anyway, I read a lot, so some people called me Professor."

"That is not why," Luis says. "It's because you, or someone who very much resembles you, left the appropriate book at the scenes of certain questionable activities."

"Appropriate book?" Ramon asks, interested now.

"*The Inferno* at the scene of an arson, *The Great Train Robbery* at, well, a train robbery. Things like that."

"And what does *la Víbora* mean?" Camden asks.

179

"The Viper," Sal answers.

"I have been told that python or anaconda would be a more apt description," Ortiz says with a wink at the women. Both Camden and Julia immediately blush. "In any case, it is clear we have travelled many varied roads, Salvatore." He looks at Camden and smiles. "Yet I have never explored a British road. An oversight that must be corrected."

"This British road has many, many tolls you must pay before you get to the end," Camden replies.

"Three pints of Guinness and a kidney pie should cover the tolls, my friend," Sal says. She glares at him.

"Jake," she says, "how much would you charge to send a wise-ass Italian to meet Jesus?"

A mischievous grin crosses Ortiz's lips.

"Jake," he says, "tell our new friends *your* street name."

"I don't have a street name, Lou," he says. "Like Sal said, that's for criminals."

"Of course you do; don't be shy."

"No."

"Ramon," Ortiz says, "what is Reverend Donovan's street name?"

"Defender of the Faith," Ramon replies with a wide smile.

Camden, Julia and Sal all turn and stare at him.

"It's a long story," he says. "Don't ask."

16

"God Bless Us Every One"

Sal knew enough about the South to not expect a white Christmas. He had, however, expected that it would at least be cold enough for a coat. Yet here it is the day after Thanksgiving—Black Friday to retailers and bargain hunters alike—and he is wearing a T-shirt with short sleeves and he is still, damn it, sweating. The store is not as crowded as he expected, given all the Black Friday hype.

"Where is everybody?" he asks Julia. "I thought this was the day of day for merchants."

"Oh, it is," she answers cheerfully, not at all concerned about the lack of customers. "Just not for us. Today is the day for marked-down electronics and other big-ticket items; you know, televisions, video game systems, stuff like that."

"Ah," he says. "And when do they come here?"

"It will pick up steadily until the week before Christmas, then we'll get slammed."

"And that's because…"

"Because last-minute shoppers, for whatever reason, buy books," she answers with the certainty of an old pro. "Maybe it's because all the good deals on other stuff have passed, or maybe because a book feels more like a present than cash or a gift card. Just watch, you'll see."

She moves away to help one of the few customers in the store, and Sal heads across the store to where Camden is rearranging a display of holiday-themed books. She seems distracted, which is odd. The girl is typically the most focused person he's ever met.

"What's wrong, cousin?" he asks when he reaches her. She looks up, almost as if she's surprised that anyone but her is here.

"Wrong?" she asks, then after a pause, "nothing's wrong."

"Whatever," he says. "Something's bothering you. Arsenal lose again?"

"Not funny," she says through gritted teeth. He takes a step back.

"Sorry," he says. "Is it the lack of customers, then? I can explain that." He is eager to show off his newfound knowledge, though he has no intention of telling her he acquired it mere moments ago.

"No," she says, pushing a small book back and forth across the corner of the display table. "Jacob told me it wouldn't get really busy until the week before Christmas."

Damn it.

"So what's the problem?" he asks, not willing to let it go until she tells him. She apparently realizes this.

"It's silly, really," she says, not looking up from the book she's still pushing across the table. "I have so much to be thankful for after all that's happened to me this year. I have a new career, new friends, and yes, even you." She manages a weak smile when she says this. "But this will be the first Christmas I've ever spent away from home, the first Christmas I won't see my mum. It's really the first time since I left that I really miss England."

"That's not silly at all," he replies. "The first time I spent Christmas away from home I was stuck in a train station in Buffalo. It really bothered me, and I'm supposed to be a tough guy." She nods, but still does not look up. "Anything I can do?"

"No," she says, finally looking at him. "It will be fine."

"What about going home for the holidays?" he asks, though he knows the answer.

"I can't afford that, and it will be our busiest time," she says, then looks around. "All current evidence to the contrary. No need to worry about me, Sal. But thanks."

She leaves the book on the corner of the table; Sal puts it back in its proper place and watches her walk to the counter. He can just hear Jacob prattling on about Dickens to a customer when an idea strikes him. If Camden can't go back to England for Christmas, maybe they can bring England to her.

A few nights later he has assembled their core group at the Dream Emporium, minus Camden. He is actually surprised that Jacob came, but it turns out his sisters-in-law are still in town following Thanksgiving and he is glad for the excuse to not be home. Heather and Julia are there as well, but Ramon had to study for a chemistry exam.

"Okay," Sal says, getting straight to the point. "Camden's never been away from home at Christmas, and it's putting her in a serious funk. So I say we bring Christmas in England to her."

"I knew there was something wrong," Heather says, "but she never would tell me what it was. But how exactly do we bring England here?"

"I've been giving that some thought," Sal says, "and I have a few ideas to run by you. And Jacob, you're going to get the ball rolling tomorrow."

"How exactly am I going to do that?" he asks suspiciously.

"She's going to ask you to be the store's Santa Claus," he replies.

"What? Where in the blazes did she get a crazy idea like that?"

"From me," Sal says with a smile. "Just do exactly as I say."

Sal lays out his entire plan. By the time he's done, everyone agrees it just might work. At the very least it will make things very interesting.

"I will not dress up as Santa Claus," Jacob says with a firm shake of his head. Sal had warned her this would be his response, but Camden thought he would at least do it for the children.

"Do it for the children," she says, not quite begging, but more than pleading.

"Children do not expect a Santa in every store they visit," he replies. "And certainly not in a bookstore. Have you *ever* seen a Santa in a bookstore?"

"Well, no," she admits. "But we need December to be a huge sales month, and Julia thinks Santa will drive sales. Black Friday has come and gone and we are nowhere near being in the black."

"I told you it wouldn't be a big day for us," he says. "Just wait."

"So what about being Santa?" she asks again hopefully.

"I'm too skinny," he says, then grins. "Make Sal do it."

"He refused already. He said his heart was three sizes too small. And cold and black. And in a box under his bed. You get the point."

"He's right on all counts," Jacob says with a chuckle. "Why don't you step outside the box on this one, Camden?

Everyone does Santa and elves and reindeer. Try something they'll talk about, that will make people show up just to experience it."

"Such as?" Her tone is skeptical.

"Dickens," Jacob replies, thinking to himself that it really was a stroke of genius on Sal's part.

"Dickens?" she repeats. With her accent she immediately reminds him of a Dickens character. "What does that mean?"

"*A Christmas Carol*," my dear. We bring Victorian London to our little corner of Texas."

"You mean Tiny Tim and the ghost of Christmas past and scary old dead Jacob Marley? Interesting that you two have the same first name," she muses.

"Cute," he says. "No, I don't mean we recreate the story. But we can recreate the time period, or at least the feel of it. The Dickens story singlehandedly resurrected the observance of Christmas in England, and America too, and that is the time in history we subconsciously associate it with."

"Um, wouldn't the time period we think of be when Jesus was actually born?" she asks.

"Absolutely not," he says. "We even view that through the lens of what Charles Dickens created."

"I suppose we could give it a try," she says hesitantly.

"Excellent," Jacob says, rubbing his hands together like Scrooge. "Trust me, this is much better than some fat old Santa."

Much to Camden's surprise, the Dickens plan actually works. Heather procured period costumes from a friend in the TCU theater department, Sal and Julia decorated the store, and Jacob pushed all his beloved dead Russian authors to the back in favor of an all-Dickens display. It was worth it just seeing Sal in a top hat every day.

The changes do indeed bring in more customers, and along with the sales comes an unexpected side benefit for Camden: a large number of British tourists, all stopping in to see if these Texans can actually recreate a Dickens Christmas. Talking to people who sound like her lifts Camden's spirits noticeably, and she grills each one for news from back home. Sal does his part after hours by keeping their television locked on BBC America, and within a week has become a closet Doctor Who fan. But the best part comes on Christmas day.

With considerable help from long-distance calls to Camden's mum, Heather and Julia have cooked a traditional English Christmas dinner. They start with shrimp cocktail (her mum calls them prawns). After this they pull out the Christmas crackers that Sal bought online, which are not a food but rather a cardboard tube wrapped in brightly colored paper. The tube has three chambers, with the middle chamber containing a tiny explosive charge so that when two people pull on each end of the cracker, it breaks with a bang.

Inside the chambers are the following: a paper crown which everyone must wear, a very small toy, and a joke containing the worst puns imaginable. It is an odd little device, but Camden is delighted.

The crackers are followed by the main course: roast turkey with chestnut stuffing, gravy, and roasted potatoes. There are also pigs in blankets, roasted parsnips thyme, sliced carrots, and (yuck) Brussels sprouts. Finally, there is an amazing dessert of Christmas plum pudding with brandy butter sauce.

When no one can eat another bite, Sal goes to his room and returns carrying a very large box with a bow on top. He sets it down in front of the television.

"Open it," he says to Camden. "It's from all of us."

She squeals with delight and rips off the wrapping paper. She lifts something out of the box; it looks like a chair.

"What's this then?" she asks, staring at what she has just unwrapped.

"It's a chair," he says. "Well, more accurately it's a chair fashioned from a stadium seat. You should recognize the color."

Her eyes widen.

"You didn't!"

"Not directly, no. Being five thousand miles from North London meant I had to hire a contractor for the job. He did quite well."

"This is really from Emirates Stadium?" she asks, her voice now more of a squeal. "It just opened in August!"

"Indeed," Sal assures her. "Home of your beloved, hapless, pull-defeat-from-the-jaws-of-victory Arsenal Football Club. Lord knows you talk about them enough. There's also a tin of dirt he dug up from near one of the goals."

"No!"

"Yes. Father Christmas must like you a lot."

Camden looks as though she might cry.

"I also borrowed some shotguns," Sal continues, "so we could go wassailing just like in Merry Olde England. Turns out it's really just a crazy word for caroling while getting hammered on hot mulled cider, so the guns are not only unnecessary but probably unwise."

At this her tears turn to laughter, which progresses to snorting, then to more laughter because of the snorting.

"And as our final salute to Christmas in England," Julia says, "we're all going to watch *Love Actually*. I never thought about it until Sal pointed it out, but it has two wizards from the Harry Potter films...Emma Thompson and Alan Rickman...and a Jedi...Liam Neeson...which he says makes it cool for guys to watch."

"I can't believe you did all of this for me," she says, starting to cry again.

"Like I've said before," Sal says, putting an arm around her. "We're one big happy dysfunctional family. Merry Christmas, Camden."

17

"Anything You Can Do, I Can Do Better"

It is early January, and Sal is arranging a display at the front of the store. It is not something he usually does, having no real aptitude for such things, but at some point during a recent night of drinking with Ortiz he challenged Camden and Julia to a contest. They would each set up a display table, and whoever's table sold the most books over a one-week period would be the winner. The winner would receive a cash prize (each of them put up $50) and the permanent title of King of All Booksellers. He supposed the title would actually be Queen if one of the girls won, but that was not going to happen. Upon hearing of the contest, Jacob and Heather each wanted in on it, so that with their $50 added to the pot, the winner would receive $200.

Jacob had quite predictably gone with the Russian authors, Heather with Hemingway, Julia with fictional female detectives (Stephanie Plum, Kinsey Millhone, Miss Marple), and Camden with a mishmash of cooking, gardening, and travel books. *The Forbidden Fruit* was strictly forbidden. Much to Jacob's chagrin, the goal was number of books sold, so the higher prices of his rare volumes were not an advantage; in the end he chose current printings of them for his table.

Sal went a different, and he was sure a winning, direction: books about books. It gave him a wide range of choices from both fiction (*The Shadow of the Wind, The Name of the Rose, The Guernsey Literary and Potato Peel Pie Society, Booked to Die*) and non-fiction (*84 Charing Cross Road, Shakespeare and Company, Used and Rare: Travels in the Book World, The Yellow-Lighted Bookshop*). He reasoned that people who took the time to actually shop in a real store rather than online had a love for bookstores and for books as objects as well as for what they contained between their pages.

He is placing *Shakespeare and Company* in the center of the display as Camden walks by. She stops and looks at his table, then at the book he is gently, almost reverently, nudging into the exact center.

"What book is that?" she asks.

"It's *Shakespeare and Company*," Sal says. "You know, the autobiography of Sylvia Beach."

"Who is Sylvia Beach?" Camden asks.

A sudden hush comes over the bookshop as every employee within earshot, including Siren One and even a few customers, turn to stare at her in disbelief. Sal is momentarily speechless himself. He points to a framed black and white photograph that hangs behind the front counter.

"That," he says finally, "is Sylvia Beach. She is the patron saint of booksellers."

Camden stares at the photograph, then seems to be thinking hard.

"I'm pretty sure," she says confidently, "that I read somewhere that the patron saint of booksellers is St. John of God."

Sal walks over and puts a hand on her shoulder, shaking his head sadly.

"How can you know the obscure saint the Catholic Church chose for booksellers and not know about Sylvia Beach? You're not even Catholic."

"I saw the saint on a quiz show or something," Cam says. "And why would I know her? I'm an accountant, remember? Or at least I was."

He thrusts the book in her hands, then walks to a different part of the store. He returns shortly with another copy and places it gently on his display table.

"Read that," he says. "You can't call yourself a bookseller if you don't know Sylvia Beach." He is about to say more when Julia yells to him from across the store.

"Sal! Telephone's for you." He walks over and takes the phone from her.

"Hello," he says.

"Is this Salvatore Terranova?" a man asks.

"Apparently. Who's this?"

"My name is Zeke Donovan," the man says. "Luis Ortiz was telling me about you, and I would like to interview you."

"Donovan?" Sal asks. "Any relation to James Donovan?"

"He was my brother," Zeke replies. "Jake and Eddie are my nephews, and Ortiz might as well be."

"I see," Sal says. "You said you want to interview me. You a reporter?"

"That and more, son. This would be a feature story."

"Uh huh," Sal says, not liking where this is going.

"Is this for TV, a magazine, what? Not that I'm actually considering it. Which, if you're James Donovan's brother you should know without me telling you."

"Oh, don't give me that *omerta* crap," Zeke says. "If you're Frank Templeton's nephew then you're not full-blooded Sicilian, and thus not a made man. You can talk to anyone you want to."

"Talking about my past could get me into some hot water."

"Look," Zeke says in a suspiciously friendly tone, "I write for the *Dallas Free Press*, not the *New York Times*. And I don't want to talk about your past as much as about your present. You know, a 'Burglar to Bookseller,' angle, something like that. A human interest piece."

"Human interest piece," Sal repeats.

"Yes. Unless you just feel like giving me the scoop on that Ithaca heist."

"I was in Scranton that night," Sal says.

At that moment Julia is walking past him. She leans over, says "Atlantic City" into the phone, and keeps walking.

"Whatever," Zeke replies. "Come on, son. It will be good publicity for your store, and quite the coup for me."

"Sorry, sir, but no."

There is silence on the other end of the line for so long that Sal thinks the man may have hung up.

"Ortiz said you'd say that," Zeke says finally. "He told me to ask if your cousin knows you're dating her best employee."

Sal glances around to be sure no one has overheard this.

"How the hell does he know that?"

"Luis is a keen observer of people, son," Zeke answers. "So why don't you come on over to downtown Dallas? My office window has an excellent view of where American history changed forever."

Sal thinks hard, but sees no way out of at least meeting the man.

"How about next Monday?" he says in a defeated tone.

"Monday will be just fine," the man agrees, then hangs up.

With less than one day left, the contest is not going well for Sal. Julia is leading, followed by Camden, Sal, and Heather. Jacob is firmly in last place. He blames this on the poor taste of the reading public in general, and on Sal's attempts at sabotage in particular.

Jacob had arrived that morning to find the following sign had been posted on his display after he left the night before; it is the third such sign in as many days:

"Don't stop at this table acting like you're going to buy one of these books, and don't protest that you read some of them in high school or college either. In high school you read the Cliff's Notes, and in college you sobered up long enough to pay a freshman to read it for you. Let's just all admit that Russian writers are simply a beating. Thanks, the Management."

From a business standpoint, Camden is less than pleased; for purposes of the contest she looks the other way. Julia and Heather find it funny. Jacob, however, is livid. For his part, Sal denies any involvement.

Camden is working the register that evening, looking over the sales totals for the contest, when an attractive woman in her 40s walks up to the register.

"Can I help you, ma'am?" Camden asks.

"Yes, you can," the woman replies. "I need fifteen copies of *The Shadow of the Wind*, please."

"Did you say fifteen copies?" Camden asks, startled by the request.

"Yes, fifteen. My book club is starting it next week."

Camden goes to the back room and gathers up fifteen of the copies that Sal had ordered specifically for the contest. She thinks it an odd coincidence, but it is still a very popular novel, especially with book clubs. And he's still well behind her in the rankings.

The woman pays for the books, thanks her, and leaves. Ten minutes later another woman enters the store and walks up to the counter.

"I need seventeen copies of *The Guernsey Literary and Potato Peel Pie Society*, please," the woman says with a smile.

"Is this for a book club, ma'am?" she asks.

"Yes, it is," the woman replies. "My reading group is finishing up our current book, and this one was highly recommended."

"Right," Camden says. "I've heard that as well."

She boxes up the books and has Ramon carry them out for the lady. *It's a coincidence,* she tells herself, *nothing more.* Perhaps Sal was simply lucky enough to pick titles that were book club favorites and it was just now paying off for him. She adds the seventeen to Sal's total; he moves past her into second place.

She is still pondering this turn of events when Julia walks up to the counter. Camden tells her what has happened and marvels at the coincidence. Julia, however, sees something more sinister at play. Before she can voice her suspicions, two more women walk up to the counter.

"Let me guess," Camden says before they can speak. "You both need books for your reading groups."

Both of the women smile and nod.

"I need twenty copies of *84 Charing Cross Road*," says one.

"I need twelve copies of *Mr. Penumbra's 24-Hour Bookstore*," says the other.

Camden stares at them in disbelief: two more of Sal's titles. Julia and Ramon gather the books as Camden rings up the sales and notes them on the contest log. Over the next hour, five more women and one man request the following books for their groups, all from Sal's table: five copies of *The Thirteenth Tale*, ten copies of *The Name of the Rose,* eleven more copies of *The Shadow of the Wind,* and eight copies of *Booked to Die.* The store closes thirty minutes later, as does the contest. The final tally shows Sal winning by thirty-five books sold.

"Unbelievable," Cam says as she looks at the final numbers. "How in the world did he do it?"

"With guile and treachery, I'm sure," Julia says bitterly.

At that moment Sal walks in, a huge grin on his face. He moves quickly to his display, and is thrilled to see it has almost no books left on it. Then he struts—yes, *struts*—up to the counter.

"How did we do tonight, ladies?" he asks innocently.

"I think you know very well how we did," Julia says. "The question is how you pulled it off."

"What do you mean, dear Julia?"

"Don't 'dear Julia' me," she says. "Spill it, Terranova."

In spite of himself, Sal starts laughing. Camden and Sal wait stoically for him to stop.

"I realized as this thing got close to ending that it's about marketing," Sal says, "and that I had not been doing an effective job of marketing my books."

"And?" Camden asks, barely controlling her irritation.

"And I decided to market directly to the numerous reading groups that patronize our fine establishment."

"How did you do that?" Julia asks, now actually interested. This is a new side of Sal.

"I called the group leaders—I discovered this morning that we have their numbers on file—and made them all a great deal. If they chose one of the books I recommended, I would not only give them 20% off the next book their group chose after this one, I would also come and speak to each of their groups personally. The ladies seemed especially happy about that part. But the books had to be purchased by tonight."

Camden and Julia look at each other, then at Sal.

"Why in the world did neither of us think of that?" Camden asks Julia. "It's probably the best idea I've heard in a long time."

"It actually is," Julia agrees. "Are you sure it was really your idea?" she asks Sal with a wink.

"Completely original," he answers. "And I cannot wait to rub it in Jacob's face tomorrow."

"I hate to say it," Camden says, "but nice job, Sal."

Sal gives her a confused look.

"Sal?" he says. "I know no one named Sal. My name is the King of All Booksellers."

He collects the money from them, bows, and then walks upstairs.

18

"Interview With A…"

Sal had never driven in Dallas before, but for as much as people bitched about the traffic it was nothing compared to Manhattan. He takes I-30 west to downtown and exits at Commerce Street. To his surprise, he finds himself driving through the triple underpass made famous by the Kennedy assassination. He makes a few more turns and pulls up to what looks like an old warehouse that has been refurbished into high-dollar lofts and some offices. Zeke told him that the offices of the *Dallas Free Press* were on the sixth floor, so he parks and enters the building. He finds the office easily, and a pretty receptionist points him toward Zeke's desk after reluctantly putting down her celebrity gossip magazine.

"Be careful," she says after he thanks her. "He's in one of his moods today."

Zeke Donovan's desk is against a window that looks directly across at the sixth floor of the old Texas School Book Depository Building, from where Lee Harvey

Oswald shot President Kennedy in 1963. The first thing Sal notices is that even for a man, Zeke does not keep the tidiest of workspaces.

Coffee mugs are everywhere, most still half-full, overflowing ashtrays (one under a 'No Smoking' sign), pictures of a man Sal assumes is Zeke with Richard Nixon, Bill Clinton, Emmitt Smith, and even Fidel Castro; Ramon would love that last one. There are two framed Pulitzer Prize awards, which is both impressive and completely out of place in this environment. There is also a large Old West-style wanted poster with George W. Bush's picture on it peppered with hundreds of pinholes.

Sal leans across the desk to look at a picture of two men and a woman; it was taken at a beach somewhere, and the men are clearly young versions of Luis Ortiz and Jake Donovan. As he straightens back up, he feels something whiz past his head. It lodges in the photograph of Bush: a small steel-tipped dart.

"Heads up, Sal," Zeke says as he walks up to the desk.

He shakes Sal's hand, then throws an air pistol on the desk and sits down. He is a large man with salt and pepper hair and lines around his eyes and the corners of his mouth. His hair is buzz-cut and his face clean-shaven. He wears faded jeans with desert combat boots and a hideous Hawaiian shirt.

"That's Ortiz in that picture, right?" Sal asks, pointing to it. "And your nephew, Jake?"

Zeke nods and sits down at the desk.

"That was taken twenty years ago during some crazy trip they took to Galveston," he says. "The woman is Jake's wife, Lori. She died not long after that picture was taken."

"Oh," Sal says. "I'm sorry to hear that." It is all he can think to say, and since the woman has been gone for two decades it seems an odd response.

"Thanks," Zeke says as if it had happened yesterday. "Not a day goes by that I don't miss that little girl. But you didn't drive all the way here to listen to an old man reminisce. Let's get down to business."

"Sure," Sal says. "But could you tell me a little about your paper first? I'd never heard of it before you called last week."

"We don't have a huge circulation," Zeke explains. "Our readers are loyal, inquisitive, and a little disturbed. In essence we are a weekly newspaper/tabloid that carries insightful political commentary and enlightening arts features supported by ads for strip clubs, methadone clinics, and male enhancement products. Those pay the bills."

"Fascinating," Sal says with a sardonic smile. "Exactly how is that likely to generate good publicity for my bookstore?"

"Have faith, my boy," he replies. "I guarantee your sales will skyrocket, or at least bump up a tad. So let's get started."

He pulls out a small Moleskin notebook and flips it open.

"We sell those in the store," Sal says. "I can get you a good deal if you need more."

"I always need more. Hemingway used these. So, where should we start?"

"You said the story was about my present, so no need for the whole Oliver Twist 'I am born' nonsense."

"True enough," Zeke says with a nod. "But obviously we need some background, otherwise how can we show your transformation from notorious hoodlum to respectable merchant of ideas?"

"Notorious hoodlum?" Sal repeats.

"Gotta catch the readers' attention right off the bat," Zeke says. "Maybe something like you escaped from the vicious cycle of crime, rehabilitation and recidivism by giving your life over to the dissemination of literature."

"Are your readers going to know what recidivism and dissemination mean without a dictionary?" Sal asks.

"Some will. So you were aligned, if that's the right word, with the Napoli Family."

"I was an Associate. Same idea though."

"Associate," he says, writing the word down.

"Just out of curiosity," Sal says. "Given who your brother was, how did you escape the life?"

"Easy," Zeke says. "I joined the Marines. What a lot of people don't know is that except for my brother and me, all the rest of the family were cops. Ironic, huh?"

"Yeah."

"I can do the back story easily enough now. Tell me how you first got interested in books."

"Refuge," Sal says.

"Say again?"

"Refuge. In my neighborhood, the public library was the only place besides the church that was neutral territory. No fights, no beefs, no hustles or cons allowed there. It was a refuge for me. Keith Richards has this great quote that sums it up pretty well, something along the lines of there being only two places that belong to the people: the church and the public library. He called the public library the great equalizer."

"I like that," Zeke says. "It's from his autobiography, right?"

"Right," Sal says. "Libraries truly are the great equalizer. I grew up in the public library, and in bookstores as well. They were a great place to escape the cold when my father had bet the money for heating oil on a horse that died in the back stretch, and a great place to explore worlds I figured a kid from Jersey would never see.

"Back then," he continues, "the library cards were made of a heavy card stock rather than the plastic, bar-coded ones we have today. The paper card would be warm in my hand when the librarian removed it from the odd-looking mimeograph-type machine that recorded my stack of selections. It was the first card I ever owned with my name on it. To this day I use it more than my driver's license, voter registration card, and credit cards combined.

"In those days, before everyone had cell phones or smartphones or iPods, the library was a quieter place. The librarians, many of whom had received their degrees in Library Science in the 1950s, enforced this silence with the zeal of a born-again monk. In fact, the only place as quiet, then or now, was the church. Perhaps this is another thing that made Keith link them in his quote."

Sal stops talking and looks over at Zeke.

"You sure you want to hear this?" he asks. "Seems a little boring now that I'm saying it out loud."

"Not boring at all, son," Zeke assures him. "Keep going."

"All right. Well, I would wander through the stacks for hours, finding gems like *The Three Investigators* series, *Treasure Island*, and authors I still read today like Dickens, Dumas, and Poe. Stumbling upon a book by accident and having it become a lifelong favorite is something that just can't be done through an Internet search. You have to see the books, touch them. That's how it started for me."

"And now?" Zeke prompts him. "What makes you want to sell them?"

"I guess the honest answer would be that I want to make a living doing something I love, and I love books.

Look, and I say this not admitting to anything, I never stole anything from anyone who couldn't afford to lose what I took. But that doesn't make it a good thing. Selling books is a good thing. Exposing people to a wider world is a good thing."

"An admirable sentiment," Zeke says, "especially in a tough retail environment."

"Fortunately, books are more than commodities. Each one of them is a portable universe, an unspoken contract between the writer and the reader, and a friend who will never let you down."

"I think you just gave me my closing sentence," Zeke says, snapping the notebook shut.

They both stand and shake hands again. As Zeke walks him to the front of the office, he has an idea.

"If you don't have to get back to the store right away," he says, "let's walk over to the Sixth Floor Museum. No better way to spend a morning than looking at Kennedy assassination artifacts."

"Why not," Sal says. "One of the few perks of owning the store is taking the occasional field trip."

Zeke nods in agreement, slaps him on the back, and steers him toward the elevator.

19

"Men Without Women"

"I think we need a girls' bonding weekend," Camden says to Sal early one Thursday morning. He is looking through a publisher's catalogue at some new releases that will be out in the next six months, and it is much too early in the day for one of Camden's crazy schemes. Only his crazy schemes ever work.

"What are you talking about?" Sal asks. "It's much too early for your crazy schemes."

"*My* crazy schemes?" Camden responds derisively. "This from the man who left a copy of *Bonfire of the Vanities* after cracking a safe in Ithaca?"

"I was in Albany," Sal replies.

"Atlantic City," Julia says as she walks by, not even breaking stride.

"Right, Atlantic City. Anyway, what the hell is a bonding weekend?"

"Simple," Camden says as if he is a backward child. "We all go to a resort or spa or something on Friday night, come back Sunday night, lots of talking and pampering and *bonding* in between. It will be good for morale."

"And exactly which girls are we talking about?"

"Julia, Heather, me, Kate—"

"Kate doesn't work for us," Sal interjects.

"She might as well, as much as she's here. And two of the Sirens."

"You don't know which ones because you don't know their names," Sal says.

"Which is exactly why we need bonding time."

"So it would be just me, Jacob, and Ramon holding down the fort for a weekend?"

"Don't think you can handle it?" Camden says with a sneer.

"Of course we can. Just not sure I want to."

"You boys got to have your little Hemingway fiasco," she says.

"It was not a fiasco, and it was not just the guys."

"Might as well have been," Julia says, walking by again, again not breaking stride.

"And when would this girls' weekend happen?" he asks.

"Starting tomorrow night," she replies. "Everything's already booked."

"In that case," Sal says, "have fun."

The Hemingway fiasco had started out, as most fiascos do, as a very good idea. In honor of Heather's birthday, they would hold a weekend-long Hemingway festival, complete with readings, screenings of films made from his books, a Papa lookalike contest like the one held every year in Key West, and of course alcohol. To give credit (or blame) where it was due, it had actually been Jacob's idea. He had wanted to do it around the time of Hemingway's birthday in July, but that date had come and gone. So he asked Heather, knowing her love of all things Hemingway, if he could use her birthday as the way to sell the idea to Camden and Sal. She was on board immediately.

He pitched the idea to Sal early one morning. Sal was, as Jacob had hoped, much too hung over to follow the stream of consciousness that Jacob dropped on him, but the Key West contest reference was enough of a clue for him to act like he was paying attention.

"A Hemingway festival?" Sal responded. The way Jacob's face lit up told him he had guessed correctly. "Fine with me. We can all get drunk and shoot skeet and run with the bulls through the Stockyards."

"Well," Jacob said, not liking where this was going. "I don't think we can re-create Pamplona, and I'm not sure about the skeet, but yes, Sal, you can get drunk."

Sal smiled and patted Jacob on the shoulder, then went back upstairs to lie down.

The weekend had, in Sal's humble opinion, gone extremely well. They sold a lot of books, enough of them by Hemingway to keep a smile on Heather's face for weeks. The one-screen art house theater down the street had given them a cut of the box office from the showings of *For Whom the Bell Tolls* and *The Old Man and the Sea*. They sold a ton of beer and wine, provided quite cheaply by the Blarney Stone, and the winner of the Hemingway lookalike contest was a dead ringer for dear departed Papa.

There were a few minor logistical issues, as always happens with any event. These were what Camden insisted on calling a "fiasco." The twenty-three would-be Hemingways (and Sal) had perhaps overindulged on Puerto Rican rum, and several (including Sal) had decided to reenact bullfights using a red-checked tablecloth as a cape and cars driving down the street in front of the shop as bulls. Only two of the men had been so much as grazed by a vehicle, and none of the injuries were serious. And the sight of all twenty-four of them singing *The Internationale* at 2 a.m. was well received until one narrow-minded right winger started screaming that it was a Socialist anthem. It wasn't; it was a Communist anthem, and there is a difference.

Sal was disappointed that their profits had been eroded somewhat when the police officer came in the last night asking if they had a license to sell alcohol. They didn't of course, and he threatened a very large fine until Sal discovered he was a reader.

"Who's your favorite author?" Sal asked.

"David Foster Wallace," the cop replied without hesitation. Sal raised an eyebrow at this, but made no comment.

"It just so happens," Sal said, "that we have a signed copy of *Infinite Jest* here in the store."

The cop's eyes lit up at this revelation, as Sal knew they would. He also knew that nothing more need be said; cops were the same the world over. Sal grabbed the book, put it in a bag, and sent the cop off into the night, illegal liquor sales forgotten and a new customer acquired. Jacob was not happy though.

"That copy was worth almost a thousand dollars," he complained. "And you just gave it to him."

"The fine would have been a lot more," Sal said, "and no one has even looked at the damn thing in months. If it will make you feel better I'll let you buy another copy."

"No," Jacob said. "It's not the book so much; it's the principle."

"Forget principle for one night, my friend. Here, have some rum."

It was a great time, but now Sal was going to pay for it by not having any of the girls working for the next three days. He calls Ramon and asks if he wants to cut class Friday and make a little extra money, which of course he does. He works the register himself, knowing Jacob has never mastered Camden's beloved computer system, and things go well, until Saturday morning at least. That is when forty moms with more than forty toddlers arrive, telling him Camden had emailed them that there would be a story time that morning.

"Story time?" he asks the woman who is obviously the Alpha Mom.

"Yes," she repeats impatiently. "Story time."

"Right. Would you excuse me for just one minute?"

Without waiting for an answer he retreats to the back room and calls Camden's cell. She answers on the third ring.

"The store better be burning down, Terranova," she says in place of a normal greeting. "I have cucumbers on my eyes, a soothing mud pack on my face, a Bloody Mary at my side, and I am very relaxed for the first time since I met you. Do not upset me."

"What the hell is story time?" he shouts into the phone. This elicits a laugh from Camden.

"That was actually Julia's idea to bring young moms into the store," she says. "Here, talk to her." There is a moment's silence, then Julia comes on the phone.

"It's very simple, Sal," she says. Her voice sounds strange, and he wonders if she also has on a mud pack that has hardened, making it difficult for her to move her lips. "There are three books set aside in the kids' section next to three stacks of the same books. Read each one to the kiddos in your most entertaining style, then try to sell copies to the moms. They get a 10% discount if they buy one today, and 15% if they buy all three. Have fun."

The line goes dead before he can fire her. He goes to the children's section before returning to the Alpha Mom and finds the stacks just as Julia described. The three titles are *If You Give a Mouse a Cookie, If You Take a Mouse to the Movies,* and *If You Give a Pig a Pancake.* Interesting titles, at least.

He walks back to the group of moms who are trying hard to keep their youngsters under control and leads them to the children's section. Once he's there he notices that a large area has been cleared for them to sit down while he reads. He assumes this is also Julia's doing.

Without any opening remarks he begins reading *If You Give a Mouse a Cookie.* At first the kids are rowdy, but soon they settle down and listen attentively. For his part, though he is irritated at first, by the fourth page he is actually enjoying the story. When he reads the final page of *If You Give a Pig a Pancake,* both he and the kids are sad it's over. He looks quickly at the author's name, finds her place on the shelf, then pulls out another in the series called *If You Give a Moose a Muffin.*

"I think we've got time for one more," he says to the kids' delight. The moms seem quite pleased as well.

When he finishes the final book, the children applaud. Some even hug him. To his surprise, they also sell every single copy of the books and he takes orders for several more, assuring the moms that the discount will still apply. As the group leaves the store Alpha Mom asks if he'll be reading again next time.

"Definitely," he says.

"Good," she says, then hustles her little one out the door, three books in hand.

Sal is at the checkout counter ordering replacement copies of the books they sold when Ramon walks over, a concerned look on his face. He looks around to be sure they are alone before speaking.

"I think we need more help in here, Mr. Sal," he says. Sal has tried to break him of the habit of putting Mister in front of his name, but has only been partially successful. For a revolutionary, the boy is polite to a fault.

"Why, Ramon?" Sal asks, looking up from the order screen on his computer. "We've done all right the past two days with just the three of us."

"Yes and no," Ramon replies. "It got pretty dicey while you were reading to the children. We had a rush while you were on *If You Take a Mouse to the Movies*—that's my favorite, by the way—and I think we're a little short in the register."

"Short? What do you mean?"

"I know computers, but I've never worked the front counter, so Mr. Jacob checked people out while I helped others find books they were looking for. But Mr. Jacob doesn't do well with technology, and he told me he couldn't get the credit card reader to work, so he improvised."

"Improvised? Don't tell me he pulled out that ancient imprint machine, the one Julia called the slide thingy? I thought we threw that away."

"We did," Ramon assures him. "No, instead of running the cards he accepted whatever cash the customer had. If the book was $20 and they only had $15, he took it. He said it's the same thing as giving the discounts we do sometimes."

Sal smacked his own forehead with an open palm, since Camden wasn't there to do it for him. He was afraid to ask the next question.

"How many customers did we have while I was doing story time?"

"Quite a few," Ramon says. "You read a long time. There were at least ten or twelve people he checked out, maybe more. Some of them had enough cash, but most didn't."

"It couldn't be helped, I suppose," Sal said, determined not to lose the good feeling from story time. "But let's not tell Camden about this, okay?"

"Certainly. Also, he didn't collect the sales tax on any of the sales."

Sal lets out a heavy sigh and shakes his head. No wonder Julia had laughed at him when he asked if Jacob ever worked the checkout counter.

"It's fine, Ramon. Thanks for letting me know."

Ramon lingers after this; clearly he has more to say. Sal waits until the silence becomes uncomfortable.

"Was there something else, Ramon?"

"Yes, sir. There is another reason I think we need more help."

"Really? What is that?"

"I think we're missing out on sales because we have a substandard fantasy and science fiction section."

"Substandard?" Sal repeats. "It's not all that large, I'll admit, but I don't think I'd call it substandard."

"That's what my friends who have come here call it. And the thing is, the people who buy in that genre, mostly young men, still buy far more printed books than e-books, for whatever reason. I know Miss Heather tries to stock it well, but she doesn't really know what we need there. Her strength is literature."

That is certainly true. And while he, Camden, Julia, and Heather all have input on what is ordered, if Ramon is right about the demographic, none of them fit it.

"So you think we need a full-time fantasy/sci-fi guru?" Sal asks. "Not sure we can afford that."

"Not full-time," Ramon says, shaking his head. "I know someone who's looking for a part-time job who would be perfect; he is the older brother of a friend of mine, and he was a few years ahead of me in school. We play video games together sometimes."

Sal considers this, and also that he should not do anything without talking it over with Camden first. Then he considers the lost revenue this morning, the possible lost sales because the section is "substandard," and finally the fact that Camden left him to run things alone while she gets pampered with mud packs and vodka.

"Have him come see me," he tells Ramon. "Today if possible."

Sal is locking the front doors when a very large man appears, apparently wanting in. Sal weighs the potential sale against how tiring the day has been, factors in how hard it would be to fight him if he actually intends to rob the place, and makes his decision.

"Sorry," he says through the glass, "but we're closed."

The man nods, but doesn't turn away. He seems easygoing, but you can never tell.

"Ramon sent me," the man says. "About a part-time job?"

Sal unlocks the door and lets the man in. Upon closer inspection, he is not only huge, but also young, early twenties at most. Once he is inside, Sal relocks the door.

"I didn't expect you to come so late," he says, trying not to sound irritated.

"Ramon told me to wait until after the store closed," the young man replies. "Something about an older gentleman not being good with computers."

Sal smiles and relaxes when he hears this. *That boy thinks of everything,* he thinks to himself. If he ever gave up dreams of revolution he'd make a great CEO someday.

"I'm Ben Williams," the man says, extending a hand the size of a catcher's mitt.

Ben Williams, it turns out, is 20 years old, sporadically attends Tarrant County College, lives with his grandparents ("they need someone around to do the heavy lifting, like Ramon does for you," he tells Sal), and requires only enough cash to keep himself in beer and sci-fi novels. To say Ben is "strapping" is an understatement; he is just short of being a Greek god. A brief conversation confirms that he is indeed an expert on science fiction and fantasy books.

"You could fill this whole store with sci-fi/fantasy and not even scratch the surface of the genres," Ben tells him. "So you have to be selective in what you stock. You have to...what's the word...?"

"Curate?" Sal ventures, having learned the word from Heather.

"That's it," Ben replies. "You have to curate the section, like in a museum or art gallery. If you carry only the best, the fans will come here. And they'll also order

222

stuff from you that you don't have in stock instead of from the Evil Empire that is Blue Nile."

"Okay," Sal agrees, having already decided to hire him, if only to increase the testosterone level of the store. "And since I'm learning this on the fly, what's one important thing about this genre I need to remember?"

"That's easy, man," Ben says. "You can never carry too much *Star Wars*. And while the *Dr. Who* fans aren't as numerous, they are rabidly committed."

Sal nods, trying to make it at least appear that he understands why this would be true. Then, before making the official offer of employment, he realizes he should ask at least one of the dreaded interview questions, just in case.

"One more question, Ben, if you don't mind."

"Shoot," Ben replies. "Two-question interviews are my favorite kind."

"What happens to vampires when they are exposed to sunlight? From a literary standpoint, not necessarily in real life." The whole point of this question is to separate the Bram Stoker fans from the *Twilight* fans.

"That depends a lot on your age, I think," he replies. "The correct answer, from both a literary and historical standpoint, is that they burst into flame, burn up and/or disintegrate into ash, and die. If you ask a kid who's only read the Stephenie Meyer *Twilight* books, they'll probably answer that they sparkle...unforgivable. Of course, someone who has only seen the film version of *Interview with the Vampire* is just as likely to say that they burn up and then Tom Cruise and Brad Pitt make out. Not quite accurate, but probably more fun for the vampire."

"Great answer," Sal says. "You start on Monday."

Sal is explaining to Camden how he came to hire Ben on the Monday the women return from their bonding weekend. Ben is furiously rearranging his new section of the store, making notes on what they need to add and what needs to go. Camden doesn't seem to hear him, though. Much like Heather, Julia, and Siren One, she is simply staring admiringly at Ben.

"Are you listening to me?" Sal asks, annoyed that she's ignoring him.

"Yes," she says in a faraway voice. "Ramon's friend...*Star Wars*...*Dr. Who*...more sales...gorgeous. I need to let you do the hiring more often."

"He's a child, for crying out loud," Sal says.

"But he's not *my* child," Camden says.

"He's almost my age," Heather adds.

"I usually like my men older," Siren One puts in, "but for him I'd make an exception."

Julia, perhaps diplomatically, says nothing.

"Well, I hate to crush the Harlequin Romance plans you ladies have for the young man," Sal says with malicious satisfaction, "but young Ben happens to be gay."

All of them turn to him in unison.

"That's a shame," Heather says. "I guess that means I shouldn't ask him to read *Green Hills of Africa* to me."

"I could turn him," Siren One says. "If I really wanted to."

"What I don't understand," Camden says, "is when I lost the ability to recognize that a man is gay."

Sal puts a reassuring arm around her.

"Don't feel bad, cousin," he says. "If he hadn't brought his boyfriend with him to fill out the payroll paperwork yesterday, I never would have believed it myself. He knows his stuff though, and that's what matters."

They all sigh, but don't stop staring. A Greek god is still a Greek god, no matter his preference. Julia suddenly looks up at Sal.

"If he's good friends with Ramon," she says, "you don't suppose that means—"

"Not a chance, Sherlock," he says, cutting off the rest of her thought. "Unless Ramon and the brunette twins he left here with Saturday night were just good friends. That boy is too much like his uncle to ever be anything but one hundred percent Puerto Rican heterosexual."

At that moment, Ben looks up from his notes and smiles at them. The women all melt into small puddles on the floor, and Sal heads to the back room for a mop.

20

"March of the Penguins"

The store is busy on a late Tuesday afternoon. Jacob is deep in conversation with a man roughly his own age about the merits of Turgenev versus Chekov. Julia and Heather are ringing up customers' purchases, and Camden is pleased to see that a small line has formed waiting to check out. Lines mean sales.

She walks over to a display of new releases Sal is organizing on a small table. Ever since he won their contest he has been of the opinion that he is something of a marketing genius.

"I wouldn't put that one here," she says, pointing to a book he has placed toward the front of the table.

"And why not?" he asks. "Surely you're not questioning the display king?"

"You did not just refer to yourself as the display king," she says. "You won one contest—"

"And was proclaimed 'King of All Booksellers'." He looks around. "Now where did I put my crown?"

"Don't be a git," she says.

"I wouldn't be if I knew what the hell that was." He continues arranging books.

"Again," she says impatiently, "that book doesn't fit there."

He puts down the book he is holding, lets out a frustrated sigh, and looks hard at her.

"Why are you breaking my balls, cousin?" he asks. "Why doesn't this particular book fit your expectations for our new release table?"

"Because it came out last year," she says.

He looks at her as if she's from another planet, or worse, England.

"Did not."

"Did too."

"Did not," he repeats firmly. "It came in this morning's shipment."

"I ordered copies because the author died last week," she explains. "Invariably people will ask for it now."

"I didn't hear anything about this guy dying," Sal protests.

"It wasn't a guy," Camden says. "In this case, Michael Zonder was a woman. And you've never even heard of her, have you?"

"Well, no," he admits. "But that doesn't mean it's a year old."

"Check the copyright page."

He hesitates, then flips open the book to the copyright page. It has the previous year's date.

"I'll be damned," he says.

Just then, a voice comes from behind them.

"You certainly will if you keep using that foul language, young man, especially in a public place."

They turn to see a diminutive woman dressed from head to toe in a black habit: a nun.

"Good morning, sister," Camden says. "I apologize for my cousin's language; we were having a small disagreement."

"That's no reason to resort to gutter talk," she says sternly. "I would expect that a gentleman who works with books would have a wider vocabulary."

Camden simply nods, then looks at Sal and is shocked by what she sees. He has gone white as a sheet, and while she expected a sharp retort to the nun's comment, Sal says nothing. She turns back to the nun.

"Can we help you find something, sister?" she asks.

"Yes," she replies, drawing a list from a pocket in her habit. Camden never knew habits had pockets. "There are several Miss Marple books I have yet to read, and I would like to see if you have them in stock."

"Ah," Camden says. "My mum used to read Agatha Christie to me at bedtime."

The sister smiles for the first time. She hands the list to Camden, who then hands it to Sal. He tries to step back, but she thrusts it into his hand.

"Sal will be happy to help you, sister," she says, giving Sal a malicious grin. "And you let me know if he uses any more bad language."

Sal's shoulders slump in defeat. He leads the nun to the mystery section and waits patiently, and silently, while she makes her selections. When she is finished she starts to walk to the register, but Sal stops her. Camden moves closer to them, anticipating trouble.

"I will pay for your books myself, sister," he says in a deferential tone Camden has never heard come from Sal's mouth, "to make up for my offensive language earlier. I hope my behavior will not make you think less of my colleagues or our store, and that you will come back soon."

To Camden's further amazement, he gives the nun something of a bow as he says this. The nun smiles pleasantly, nods, and pats him on the shoulder. He flinches slightly when she touches him.

"Thank you very much, young man," she says as he places the books in a bag and hands them to her. She nods quickly to Camden and strides purposefully to the front door. She stops before exiting and walks back to Sal, who tenses even more visibly.

"Are you by any chance a Catholic, young man?" the nun asks him bluntly.

"Yes, sister, I am." His tone is almost apologetic.

"I see," she says, her own tone once again disapproving. "Then be sure to tell the priest about your language when you go to confession this weekend. You do go to confession, correct?"

"Of course, sister," he answers quickly while moving her toward the door again. "This week for sure."

Satisfied with her accomplishments both commercial and spiritual, the nun leaves the shop without another word. Sal stands outside and watches her walk down the sidewalk, relaxing a little more as each step takes her farther away.

As they are closing up the store that night, Camden brings up the encounter with the nun. Much to Sal's annoyance, she recounts the entire episode for Julia, Ramon, and Jacob. To Sal's further annoyance, they all laugh as she tells it, except Ramon, who glances at Sal with something that seems like understanding.

"Is our big, bad gangster afraid of a little nun?" Julia asks in a baby-talk voice.

"No," he says, more sharply than he intended. "I am not afraid of a little nun."

"I am," says Ramon, "even more than I am of clowns. Uncle Luis says nuns are God's storm troopers. He says twelve of them held off three Panzer Divisions that were attacking the Vatican during World War II. Very tough ladies."

Everyone, including Sal, looks at him trying to decide if he is serious, at least about the Panzer Divisions.

"I know it sounds crazy, and you probably never heard about it," he says. "But Uncle Luis was in Special Operations during his Army time, so he knows stuff regular people don't."

They all continue staring for a moment, then turn back to Sal.

"I get you being leery of them," Jacob says. "I'm not Catholic, but even I know what a holy terror they were, at least back in my day. But I thought your generation came up under the kinder, gentler Church."

"The lucky ones did," Sal says. "I wasn't one of the lucky ones."

"What does that even mean?" Camden asks.

"It means that the penguins at my school were not kind and gentle," Sal says.

Julia has burst out laughing, though Sal was not smiling when he said it.

"Penguins?" she asks once she has stopped laughing. "Did you really just call the nuns penguins?"

"I damn sure did," he says defensively. "Tell me she didn't look like a penguin in that getup. A mean, angry little penguin."

Now everyone is laughing, including Ramon, which only flusters Sal more.

"You Protestants just don't get it," Sal says. "No offense, Ramon."

"None taken, sir. I have rejected all forms of religion to purely follow the revolution. But don't tell my mother."

"Then explain it to us," Camden says, still laughing.

"Fine," Sal says, "but I still don't expect you to understand. It's something you had to actually live through to comprehend, like a war or an asteroid wiping out all life on Earth. Anyway, to Jacob's earlier comment, at my school the nuns were not 'liberated' as many became after Vatican II. They still wore the habit, which as I pointed out made them look like giant penguins.

"They still believed strongly that any child who made it through school with less than three permanent scars (physical, not mental...there were far more than three of those) had no chance of entering Heaven. I, for example, have several scars across my knuckles from a large metal ruler, one near my scalp from when my 5th grade teacher flipped over a desk with me still sitting in it, and a broken nose from a punch thrown by my 6th grade teacher. It was actually the same nun from 5th grade; she had moved up with us for some reason. To be fair, I guess I did punch her first."

"You punched a nun?" Camden exclaims. "Why in the world would you do something like that?"

"The whole thing remains fuzzy in my memory," Sal says. "I think it started with a comment I made about her beard. Anyway, with one slap she dropped me like a sack of flour. I hopped right up and punched her square on the jaw. Her head did not even move. I think the woman had been the Golden Gloves middleweight champ of Milwaukee in 1957.

"She must have hit me again, because the next thing I remember is being home with my mom lecturing me about laying my hands on the nuns, who were the brides of Christ, and how that would send me to Hell if I didn't repent. I personally thought Christ's bride would look more like Farrah Fawcett than Joe Frazier in a black dress, but Mom was insistent. So yeah, like Ramon I'm scared of penguins to this day…won't even go near that part of the zoo."

"That is the craziest story I've ever heard," Julia says, clearly loving it. "So school was basically a nightmare for you."

"Not all of it," Sal says. "High school was better in almost every way."

"How so?" Jacob asks. "Did you escape to public school?"

"No," Sal says, "but my high school was run by the Salesians, an order of priests founded by St. Frances de Sales."

"I've never heard of them," Camden says.

"Most haven't," Sal says. "They don't have the public relations skills of the Jesuits or the Franciscans. But they were as laid back as could be, unlike the Jesuits who taught some friends of mine at a school across town."

"Laid back?" Julia asks, surprised.

"Yeah. While we were having masses with drums and electric guitars, they were chanting in Latin. While they wore suits and ties, we wore casual clothes, and even jeans if we were willing to pay three dollars a week; the money supposedly went to an orphanage in Gambia, so it was a win-win."

"No nuns?" Camden asks. Sal shakes his head.

"Not a penguin in sight for four glorious years. Also, while the Jesuit school was all boys, we had girls. My friends there may have graduated knowing how to perform 35 different types of torture—the Jesuits did bring us the Spanish Inquisition, after all—but we came out knowing how to unclasp a bra strap with one hand. Frances de Sales would have been proud."

"Sal, Sal, Sal," Camden says, shaking her head.

"The worst part of today," Sal says, ignoring her, "is that now I have to go to confession this weekend. It's been years; it will take hours."

"You don't have to go just because you told the nun you would," Camden says. "She'll never know."

"The hell she won't," Sal says firmly. "She'll know. And she'll come back here. And next time she might even bring friends. It's just not worth taking the chance."

Everything has been done for the end of the day, and Sal walks Julia to the front door.

"One thing is certain," she says as he holds the door for her.

"What's that?" he asks.

"Penguins or no penguins, you are a strange and interesting man."

21

"Bless Me, Father"

That Saturday afternoon Sal is trudging reluctantly up the steps of St. Jude Catholic Church in Arlington. He had promised the penguin he would go to confession, and he was going to keep his promise, but he would do it his own way.

He couldn't remember the last time he'd gone to confession, but it was at least ten years ago. Given all that had occurred in that time, there was no way was he going to walk down the street to St. Joseph's Cathedral and talk to a priest he might run into on the street every day. After a few phone calls he discovered there was a very understanding and very discreet priest at St. Jude's. It was worth the drive to Arlington to get that combination.

When he spoke to Father Boyle and explained his somewhat unorthodox situation, the priest told him to come an hour before the normal time for confession. That would give them time to talk—he had actually said "have an unhurried conversation"—before anyone else arrived.

Sal arrived even earlier, wanting to reacquaint himself with being inside a church again.

Upon walking into the church, Sal is immediately pleased with his choice. He hadn't known what to expect from the Texas version of a Catholic church, but this one was almost a carbon copy of St. Anthony's back in his old neighborhood. There is something to be said for familiarity when you're about to bare your soul, at least to the degree he intends to.

Sal crosses himself with holy water as he enters the church and is encouraged that he does not immediately burst into flames. The church—he vaguely remembers that the part he's in right now is called the nave, which is a strange word—is dimly lit. It is cool inside, and there is the faintest smell of incense, probably soaked into the wood from thousands of earlier Masses. The scent calms him somehow.

He walks to a side altar where a statue of the parish's patron saint stands surrounded by votive candles in red holders. He pulls out a quarter and drops it in the money box, then decides that's not nearly enough. He pulls out his wallet, folds a ten-dollar bill several times and pushes it through the slot, then lights one of the candles.

"Trying to buy some extra favor from St. Jude?" a voice behind him asks.

Sal turns around and sees a priest he assumes is Father Boyle. The man has a youthful appearance that makes it hard to guess his age, which is likely close to sixty. He is average height but solidly built, with thick salt and pepper hair and Clark Kent glasses.

"I'll take any advantage I can get, Father," Sal says, extending his hand. "Sal Terranova. Thanks for meeting me."

"As you've probably guessed, I'm Father Boyle," the priest says, shaking his hand warmly. "Meeting people is what I do. Can I assume from your accent, which was less obvious on the phone, that you're not a native Texan?"

"New Jersey," Sal says. "Just moved down here recently."

"I'm originally from Boston myself," Father Boyle replies. "Though I've been here so long I can say 'park' now instead of 'pahk'. So, would you like to come over to the rectory and talk about what's on your mind?"

"If it's all the same to you, Father," Sal says, glancing around the church, "I'd rather do this the official way."

"Certainly," the priest says with a smile. "The confessionals are right over there."

Father Boyle points to a front corner of the church, and Sal follows him. There are three identical doors set into the wall; the two outer doors each have a little white and red light bulb above them, just like back home. White means the confessional box is empty, red means someone is inside. Boyle goes through the middle door, Sal the one on the right.

Sal kneels down, fighting off a sudden panic attack this small space has given him since he was in second grade. A small door in the wall in front of him opens, and he is once again face-to-face with Father Boyle. He is startled, and apparently it shows.

"Open confession is on the right side," Father Boyle says with a hearty laugh. "If you want the screen between us you'll have to go over to the left side."

"No, this is fine," Sal says, then quickly makes the sign of the cross. "Bless me, Father, for I have sinned. It's been a really long time since my last confession."

"And what are your sins, my son?"

"Well," he replies, hesitating. "As you can imagine, there are a lot of them. Can I maybe hit the high spots?"

"Certainly," the priest responds. "We probably don't have time for you to list ten years' worth of sins, even if you could remember them all. We'll just assume the fact you're here now is evidence of your contrition and intent to amend your ways."

"Right, amend my ways. Let's see, it's been a good while since I stole anything, which is kinda freaking me out a little, but since my last confession I've stolen a lot."

"Can you clarify what 'a lot' means, Sal?"

"I don't think I can, Father. But it's a lot. It's what I do...did...and I was really good at it."

"I see," the priest says, trying to contain a grin at the misplaced pride Sal still shows. "And among the things you stole, I understand there was a particularly infamous incident in, I think, Albany."

"Actually, to be totally honest it was Ithaca," Sal says, surprised that the priest knows about this, "but if you were to ever break the seal of the confessional I'd swear I was in Brooklyn that night."

"Funny, Crime TV said your alibi was that you were in Atlantic City."

"Damn...oh, sorry for that one too, Father. And while we're on the subject of my language, I said 'damn' in front of a nun a few days ago. That's why I'm here, actually; she made me come."

"She made you come?"

"Okay, she told me I'd better come, and I have a long-standing fear of disobeying the sisters."

Father Boyle cannot contain himself and actually does laugh at this.

"We all do, son," he says. "We all do."

Sal nods, then hesitates, unsure what else to say.

"Are you married?" the priest asks.

"Married? No, Father, not married. Why?"

"Well, you're a young man, and if you're not married I have to wonder if pre-marital sex might be a problem for you."

"A problem?" Sal repeats, confused. "No, I do okay with the ladies."

"That's not exactly what I meant," the priest replies.

"Oh, right. Sorry again. Yes, Father, I have engaged in premarital activities, so to speak."

"But no adultery, correct?"

"Adultery? No, Father, we just talked about me being unmarried."

For the first time Father Boyle appears exasperated. He rubs his temples and tries again.

"And were all of the ladies you had 'activities' with also unmarried?"

"Oh, I get it," Sal says, feeling like an idiot. "Yes, all unmarried, absolutely. Though there was a misunderstanding with someone's mother."

"Say again?" the priest says, now confused himself.

"It probably doesn't qualify as a bigger sin with the Church," Sal says, "but I kind of, um, had relations with the mother of the head of the Garrafolo Family in Philly."

Father Boyle is not sure how to respond to that, so he nods and tells Sal to continue.

"I mean, it's not like she was ancient or anything. In fact, she's probably barely fifty years old and looks thirty. Nicky's one of the youngest Dons in decades; he's younger than me. It was an honest mistake."

"I see," Boyle says. "Then wouldn't the misunderstanding be *about* someone's mother, not with her?"

"You would think so, but not in this case. Nicky didn't care; I'd kicked lots of cash up to him the last year or so, and he wasn't going to kill the golden goose, but Lorraine was another story."

"I don't understand."

"When I found out she was Nicky's mother I broke it off. She wasn't happy about that."

"But if he didn't care, what could she do?" This was becoming the strangest confession he had ever heard, which was saying something.

"An angry Sicilian woman can make life very difficult when she wants to. It made the decision to move here much easier."

"And why do you think this sin is worse than the others?"

"Isn't there something in the Old Testament about sleeping with a guy's mother?"

Father Boyle ponders this for a long moment, then realizes what Sal is thinking of.

"No," he says, "there's nothing specifically about that. I think you are remembering, or mis-remembering Leviticus 18:17. It says you are not to have sexual relations with a woman and her daughter."

"Well, that's a relief," Sal says. "I've never done anything like that."

"I'm impressed that you knew the passage from Leviticus, if not quite correctly. Do you still read your Bible, son?"

"Not like I should, but yes, I still do sometimes."

"Keep it up," the priest says, then looks at his watch. "It's almost time for Mass. We should probably wrap this up."

Sal rattles off a list of more minor sins...missing Mass a couple hundred times, not paying taxes, lusting after the Sirens. He does not include pulling his gun on Randal, as that was obviously not a sin. Father Boyle prays over him and gives him absolution. Sal waits with some anxiety to hear his penance.

"For your penance," the priest says, "I want you to read one chapter from St. Luke's gospel each night until you've finished it. Then do the same with each of the other three gospels. Also, since you probably can't make direct restitution on what you've stolen over the years, I want you to find other ways in which to give back to those in need. Finally, you have to stay for Mass tonight."

"No five thousand Hail Marys?" Sal asks, surprised.

"I think this will have a better result," Boyle says gently. "But since you want to be old-school, say twenty before Mass starts."

He makes the sign of the cross over Sal, then they leave the confessional. Before leaving to prepare for Mass, Father Boyle places a hand on Sal's shoulder.

244

"Sal," he says, "you know you didn't come here because a nun scared you, right?"

"I didn't?"

"No. I think you're here because you're looking for a place to call home."

"With all due respect, Father," he says, "I think I've found my home. It's a bookstore."

"And what is the best-selling book of all time, Sal?"

"Good point, Father," Sal says with a smile.

Just before Mass starts, right after Sal has finished his twenty Hail Marys, Father Boyle appears at his pew. He hands something to Sal: a St. Jude medal on a silver chain.

"The patron saint of hopeless causes," the priest says. "To remind you that you are *not* a lost cause. It has already been blessed."

"Thanks, Father," Sal says, slipping the chain over his head. "Thanks for everything."

22

"The Last Supper"

It is another fine day of bookselling at The Last Word. The staff goes about their duties: helping customers, stocking shelves, and extolling the virtues of dead Russian authors (only one employee actually does this). Sal looks up from an order sheet he is filling out to see a delivery driver struggling to get a large parcel—more of an odd-shaped crate, really—through the front door. He hurries to the door to help the man.

"Who's this one for?" he asks once they have the crate through the door.

"A Salvatore Terranova," the man answers. "He here? I need his signature."

Sal hesitates, pondering what the box might contain and whether he might not actually want it.

"He's..." Sal starts to say.

"Sal," Camden yells from the back of the store, "I need your help when you're done."

The driver raises an eyebrow.

"He's..." Sal says again, "me."

The driver smiles as Sal signs. Once he leaves, Sal starts opening the crate. It is rectangular: long and tall but not particularly deep.

"Sal! I need help," Camden yells more loudly.

"In a sec," he says, but not loudly enough for her to hear him.

The shipping label says USDOC – Atlanta, but this doesn't register until he sees it again on the packing manifest: the United States Department of Corrections – Atlanta. Someone has sent him something from prison. He reaches into the crate after removing the packing material and feels what can only be a frame, the kind for a picture or painting, and it is big. He calls Julia over to help, and together they lift the painting gently out of the crate.

Once it is out of the crate and leaning against the front counter, all he and Julia can do is stare at it. The canvass is roughly ten feet long by four feet high. It is a painting of Da Vinci's *The Last Supper*. This version, however, has one major difference.

"What in the name of all that is good and holy is *that?*" Camden asks as she comes over to where they are standing.

"It seems to be *The Last Supper*," Julia says hesitantly. She starts to say more but then stops.

"Of course it's *The Last Supper*," Sal says. He looks as if he is about to cry. "He remembered my birthday..."

"What?" Camden says, turning to face him. "Your birthday was last month."

"Stuff moves slowly out of the penal system," he replies, "whether person or object."

"So a prisoner sent you a painting for your birthday?"

"Yep, an old friend from the neighborhood."

"He's not very good," Camden says in her matter-of-fact way. "That doesn't look anything like Jesus."

Sal stares at her in amazement.

"Jules," he says, "I'll give you twenty bucks right now if you can tell my cousin why that is."

Cam looks back and forth between them, confused.

"Because it's not Jesus," Julia answers, "at least not technically. It's Bruce Springsteen, and the apostles are all E Street Band members."

"Right you are," he says, handing her a twenty-dollar bill. "It's Nicky's specialty, putting different characters in this painting—the Rat Pack, New York Yankees, Boston Terriers—but he's never done Bruce before, and he did it for my birthday. I need to send money to help with his appeals."

"And what in the world are you going to do with this gaudy thing?" Camden asks.

"I'm gonna hang it in the shop, of course."

"You are not."

"Hide and watch me, your majesty. Hide and watch me."

Later that day, Sal is standing with Ramon and Jacob admiring the painting. It has been moved away from the counter to the far side of the shop, but does not yet hang on a wall. That battle continues.

"So besides Bruce, who are the people in place of the apostles?" Ramon asks.

Before Sal can answer, Jacob steps forward and begins pointing at the figures on the canvas.

"Obviously that's Bruce in the middle where Jesus would be," he says. "Then to his right you have Patti, Steve, Danny, Garry, Nils, and David Sancious. To his left are Clarence, Max, Roy, Vini 'Mad Dog' Lopez, Soozi, and, I think, Ernest 'Boom' Carter. He only played on one song that was ever released, but that song was *Born to Run*, so he deserves to be here." Jacob turns back to them; both are staring at him, stunned.

"How in the world did you know that?" Sal demands.

"Do the math, son," he says with a smile. "I wasn't always an old relic. The last few years I was in the Navy I was stationed at the Brooklyn Naval Yards, was in my late-thirties, and liked rock and roll. I saw him play after each of the first two albums came out, and have been a fan ever since...though I don't much like the recent political stuff."

"I...I...I can't believe it," Sal stammers. "You are my new hero."

"Then try this on for size," Jacob says. "You know that poster you have up in your office for the Bottom Line shows in August of 1975 promoting the release of the *Born to Run* album?"

"Yes."

"I was at three of them."

Sal just stares for a moment, then steps over and envelops the old man in a bear hug.

"Franklin was my uncle," Sal says, "but you are definitely a soul brother. I saw him twice at Giants Stadium, but I was up in the nosebleed section both times."

Ramon stares uncomfortably at them, then says "I'll give you two some time alone," and slowly backs away.

As Sal and Jacob continue their Bruce-inspired bromance, Camden is still fighting with what she asked Sal for help with earlier in the day. She has organized a display of staff picks in a section along the back wall, and the recessed lighting at the top of the shelf unit is out. Try as she might, she simply cannot get the old bulbs out so they can be replaced.

She knows she should ask Ramon; after all, this is part of his job. But she thinks she would look less than competent if she admits she can't even change a bulb. At one point in the process, she lost her footing, slipped off the ladder, and found herself hanging from the inner ledge where the lighting was, with her toes barely touching a lower shelf. That was the first time she yelled for Sal.

Ramon passes and notices her predicament, realizing she will not ask for help. He makes a quick decision.

"Mr. Jacob needs to see you, ma'am," he tells her.

When she walks away he scurries up the ladder, replaces the bulbs, and is gone before she returns. She looks around for him to tell him Jacob did not want to see her, then looks up and sees the lights are in place and burning brightly. She shakes her head and smiles, then puts the ladder away.

Late that night, after the shop has closed, two figures dressed completely in black enter the store. They move silently around the room for several minutes, removing items from the wall behind the counter. They lift something large to the wall, and the sound of power tools echo through the empty shop. Nothing is taken, but as they exit the shop it is clear that one of the men is considerably older than the other.

When Camden enters the store the next morning she stops dead in her tracks. For a moment she cannot speak, but this inability quickly ends.

"Sal!!" she screams, scaring staff and customers alike, all of whom are gathered around the checkout counter, staring at the painting of an E Street *Last Supper* that now hangs on the wall behind the counter. It has appeared as if by magic during the night.

The battle to remove/keep the painting rages for some time, with each side sniping at the other through comments about the painting. At one point, Camden even convinces the Archbishop of Fort Worth to come down and condemn it. Sal gives him an armload of free Robert B. Parker novels when he says he actually likes it.

"Oh, for fuck's sake," is all Camden has to say.

Early one morning the next week ("early" by Sal's reckoning at least), Camden is yelling for him to come downstairs. He gets up, still wearing the same clothes from the previous day; he had fallen asleep in them. He enters the shop from the apartment and walks to the front, only to see Jacob deep in animated conversation with four people: three men and a woman. The woman has red hair. As he moves closer, he can see they are looking at and talking about the painting. He can also now clearly see who the three are: Clarence Clemons, Little Steven Van Zandt, Patti Scialfa, and Bruce Springsteen.

In his joy and surprise he rushes over to them. For an awkward moment Bruce simply stares at Sal's shirt; it has

Bruce's face on it, circa 1978, with the words "The Only Boss I Answer To" under the picture.

"Nice," Bruce says finally. "I have one just like it, but with *her* face on it." He gestures toward Patti, who smiles and nods.

Once Jacob introduces him, he lets out a stream of typical fan platitudes before realizing they keep looking up at the painting.

"Is something wrong?" Sal asks with complete sincerity.

"Well..." Steven says.

"Actually..." Clarence says.

"It's not that we're not flattered..." Bruce says.

"But he ain't Jesus, son," Patti says with a laugh. "Trust me. And why am I in the place of the apostle John?"

"You see," Steven says, "there are many who believe that it was not John at that spot in the painting, but rather Mary Magdalene. In the original it does look like a female, but that's a bunch of nonsense."

"Like I said," Bruce says again, "it's not that we're not flattered, but it seems a little...what's the word..."

"Over the top?" Steve asks.

"Gaudy?" Patti offers.

"Tacky?" Camden says.

"Amazing?" Sal says.

"Sacrilegious," Bruce says finally. "That's the word."

"This from the man who sang about bald pregnant nuns on his first album," Clarence whispers to Sal. But Sal is crestfallen, having in essence been rebuked by his greatest hero.

"I'll get Ramon to help me take it down when he comes in," Sal says in a defeated tone. "I don't think there's space to hang it in my room, so I'm not sure what to do with it."

Bruce has continued staring at the painting.

"You know," he says, "while it is certainly sacrilegious, it is also just the thing to torment our children with. We should hang it in one of their rooms."

"Uh, maybe one of the barns," Patti replies, not liking where this is going.

"No," he says. "Definitely in the house. Maybe even the living room."

"We'll see," she says, patting him on the shoulder. "You haven't even asked Sal if he'll sell it. After all, it was a birthday present from an old friend."

"And one that's incarcerated to boot," interjects Steve.

Bruce ponders this for a moment; Sal says nothing. He still cannot believe that Bruce is in his shop.

"So what would you take for it?" Bruce asks. "I have a Fender Telecaster I played during *The River* sessions; if I signed it that would be a fair trade, don't you think?"

"Absolutely," Sal says, shaking Bruce's hand.

"Thank God," says Camden, who has been hoping for exactly this sort of outcome.

"All right," Bruce says. "We've got to be on our way, but it was great meeting you and finding this fine work of art. I'll send someone by to pack it up next week, and they'll bring the guitar at the same time."

"Where are your manners?" Patti asks, poking him in the ribs. "The guy's from back home, after all."

"Right," Bruce says. "Be sure to look us up if you're ever back in Jersey."

"Don't worry," Sal says. "I have to steer clear of the entire Northeast for a while."

"Why's that?" asks Steve.

"Misunderstanding with someone's mother," Sal answers.

"Been there," Bruce says. "That was the whole inspiration for *Rosalita*."

Steve and Clarence nod in agreement as they walk out of the shop. Sal strides over to Camden, who is trying to look busy. "I don't know how you got them here," he says with a menacing tone that quickly transforms into a huge grin, "but thanks."

"Don't mention it," she says. "Tramps like us, and all that."

23

"Always a Cop Around When You Don't Need One"

The lunch rush, if you could call it that, has thinned. Taking advantage of the lull, Sal and Julia are in the True Crime section sorting and shelving some newly-arrived backlist titles. A well-built Hispanic man in a suit enters the store and looks around. He does not seem to be looking for a book, or even at any of the books he passes on his way to the front register. He stops at the checkout counter, crosses his beefy arms across his chest, and waits. Julia hops up and hurries over to him.

"Can I help you, sir?" she asks.

"I'm looking for Salvatore Terranova," the man replies with an official-sounding tone.

Julia hesitates. In Sal's former line of work, guys in suits were either cops or hit men. She doesn't like either of these options.

"He's, well, he's..."

Sal approaches the man from behind. His posture is casual, but his eyes are not. The man does not sense his approach, which makes Julia think he is not a mob hitter. From all she has read, those guys never let someone sneak up on them.

"He's right here," Sal said. "How can I help you, detective?"

The man spins around, surprised both by Sal's quick appearance and the fact that he has already tagged him as a cop. He shows him the ID anyway, though he is thrown off just a bit. The card says Det. Michael Garcia.

"I'm Detective Garcia with the Fort Worth Police Department. Is there somewhere we can talk?"

"Right here is fine with me," Sal says.

The detective looks quickly at Julia, clearly not wanting to have this conversation in front of her. Finally he shrugs and removes a small notebook from his pocket.

"Suit yourself," Garcia says. "We've had a string of burglaries in the Westover Hills area, and our investigation led us to some similar incidents in New York and New Jersey. A call to some of the departments there brought up your name, and the fact that you had relocated here."

"I was nothing more than a person of interest in those cases, Officer. It's true I was questioned a few times, but nothing was ever proven, since there was nothing to prove."

The detective looks unconvinced. "And the Ithaca thing?"

"For Christ's sake, I was in Albany..."

He looks at Julia, who shakes her head.

"Buffalo..."

Another shake of the head.

"Atlantic City..."

A nod and a smile from Julia.

"Right," he says confidently. "I was in Atlantic City that whole night. And I have committed no crimes in your fine city, Detective. I'm just a bookseller."

Detective Garcia is not quite sure what just happened, or if this comedy of errors was staged by Sal and Julia simply to break his balls, but he lets it pass. He doesn't even know where Ithaca is, let alone care about it.

"Look, I don't care about Ithaca or New Jersey or anything but Fort Worth. Just be aware that you're on our radar now. We won't tolerate any Mafia goons pulling shit in our city."

Sal laughs out loud.

"With all due respect, Officer, the Mafia goons have been running your city since before JFK was shot. And I've been here nearly a year; your radar seems a bit slow."

"I'm not joking, Mr. Terranova. Just watch yourself. Stick to selling books and we'll have no issues."

Sal stares icily at the man, but nods. The conversation is over, but not without the typical cop tough-guy routine. Jersey or Texas, cops are the same everywhere. Garcia stares back, but then his expression softens.

"For what it's worth, I was sorry to hear about your uncle," he says. "He was a good man. Try to be more like him."

The detective is barely out the door when Julia turns on Sal. She moves close to him, but definitely not in an affectionate way. In fact, it is the first time Sal has seen her really angry.

"Is what he said true?" she demands. "Did you rob those places, Sal?"

Sal tries to smile and make light of the question.

"I'm not sure I should answer that without my lawyer present."

Julia is not amused. She pushes him hard in the chest.

"Answer me. Did you?"

Now Sal is getting angry himself. No one pushes him, not even a girl half his size. He answers her through gritted teeth, trying to keep his tone conversational.

"I'm not saying I did, but with how business was going not long ago, books sure weren't what paid the bills."

"No more, you hear me? I will not work with a criminal. And I definitely won't date one."

He glances around to see if anyone heard this last part.

"Jules, you knew I was a criminal when I got here."

"*Were.* Past tense. 'New lease on life,' remember? Or was that just bullshit?"

Somehow, hearing himself quoted by someone who actually wanted nothing more than what was best for him defuses any anger he has built up. This is unfamiliar territory for him.

"No," he says. "It wasn't bullshit."

"All right then. From now on, we sink or swim without your special fundraising skills. Deal?"

"Deal."

"Good," she says, everything right with the world again. "Dinner at my place tonight?"

24

"A Misunderstood Mother"

It is rare for all of the staff to be on duty on a Thursday night, but this is no ordinary Thursday night. Through an analysis that is as much alchemy as accounting, Camden and Sal have determined that there needs to be a seismic shift in the inventory that the store carries, and this shift requires all hands on deck if they are to be ready for the weekend.

Entire sections will be eliminated in this restructuring, from all of the science and math to automotive repair to foreign language instruction. These have been very small selections from the start, but much to Ben's delight they will be jettisoned completely in favor of more science fiction/fantasy titles.

"We have sold exactly zero math books in the last year," Camden says.

"Big shock," Sal replies.

Gardening will remain, biographies will be reduced, and all sports not baseball or golf removed. The history section will switch its focus to military history and volumes with pictures and maps. The computer science section will be replaced by poetry and local authors.

Not all of the proposed changes are accepted cheerfully, however. Though Jacob's rare and collectible area will be only slightly altered to allow for more current fiction, he is vociferous in his opposition.

"Why not just throw me out in the street and get it over with?" he asks when his most recent objection is overruled.

"Because we love you," Camden replies without a hint of sarcasm. "In fact, we are looking at renovating the store next year and creating a completely separate room for your section."

Jacob's jaw drops.

"A separate room?" he asks in astonishment. "With walls and a door? You mean a real rare book room of my own?" He sounds like a child who has been given his own bedroom after years of bunking with unruly younger siblings.

"That is our hope, yes," she says. "Sal suggested it, and I think it's a fine idea."

This puts an end to Jacob's objections.

The process of reorganizing the store actually begins well before closing time, but it is a slow night and thus not very disruptive to the few customers who come and go. Thirty minutes before closing time, three men enter the shop;

they do not look like the type who read. One is in his late-20s and wears a suit that clearly cost several thousand dollars. He has an olive complexion and his hair is perfect in a way that only weekly trips to a salon can achieve. His eyes are hidden behind dark sunglasses; he is obviously the leader of this small band.

Flanking him are two much larger men in much cheaper suits. They have faces that have seen the impact of fists thrown in anger more than once, and they scan the store with practiced precision. They also wear dark glasses.

"I am looking for Salvatore Terranova," the leader says in a voice much softer than you would expect.

Julia's stomach tightens. She knows these men are definitely not police officers, and the alternative is not good. Before she can speak, a voice comes from behind her.

"Nicky Garrafolo," Sal says, walking straight past her and up to the man. "What the hell are you doing in Texas?"

"I could ask you the same thing, my friend," he answers. He does not extend his hand or make any other move toward Sal. He simply nods to one of his companions, who turns back and opens the front door.

An attractive woman strides through the door, looking around quickly. She could be anywhere from mid-30s to mid-50s; it is simply impossible to tell. When she sees Sal, her dark eyes flash with fury.

"So there you are, you son of a bitch," she growls, moving within inches of him. Sal holds his ground.

"Hello, Lorraine," he says pleasantly. "How've you been?"

"How have I been?" she repeats, her voice growing louder. "You mean, how have I been since you ran out on me?"

"We have discussed this, Lorraine," Sal says, his tone level. "You never told me Nicky was your son."

"And that matters why, exactly? Because I'm not as young as you thought?"

"Again, that has nothing to do with it. The fact that your son is the head of the biggest Family in Philly does matter, though. Surely you can see that."

"I most certainly cannot see that," she replies. "I don't answer to him. I'm his freaking mother, for Christ's sake."

"But I did answer to him, at least when I did business in Philadelphia. That made the situation a little uncomfortable. Plus it could be seen as disrespectful to Nicky."

"Whatever," Lorraine says with a dismissive wave. "You apparently don't care about disrespecting me."

"I explained everything to you," Sal says, his exasperation showing through his calm exterior.

"Right," she says sarcastically. "No sleeping with the Don's mother, blah blah blah."

As this back-and-forth continues, Julia moves over to where Ramon and Ben are standing. If there is going to be trouble with Nicky and his men, they are the only help Sal will have. She whispers something to Ben, who smiles and nods. Suddenly Camden appears from the back and walks quickly to Sal's side.

"What is going on here?" she asks.

"I'm handling it," Sal replies.

"Is this what you threw me over for?" Lorraine asks, looking Camden up and down. "A scrawny English bimbo? I expected better from you, Sal."

"Wait just a minute!" Camden yells. She starts to move toward Lorraine, but Sal holds her back.

"Actually, this is my cousin," he says. "You need to apologize. And leave."

"Apologize hell," she spits back at him. "And I'm not going anywhere until I find out which one of these bitches is so great you'd choose them over me. Maybe the librarian over there?" She gestures toward Julia.

Sal looks to Nicky for help, but he simply smiles and shrugs his shoulders.

"Fine," Sal says. "If it will get you to stop causing a disruption in my store—"

Before he can say another word, Ben is at his side. He places his hand on Sal's shoulder.

"She's not going to understand, Sally," he says in a feminine voice that Sal has never heard before. He then gently strokes Sal's hair.

Sal stares at him, unable to respond. Behind Lorraine, Nicky is smiling more broadly. Lorraine's eyes widen as she grasps what Ben means.

"Oh my God!" she exclaims. "You're gay!"

"Lorraine—" Sal tries to interrupt, to no avail.

"It makes total sense," she continues. "I knew the whole thing about offending Nicky was crap. You left me because you like guys. Well, I'm good, but even I can't compete with that."

Without another word she turns and walks out the door, one of the goons following behind her. Sal steps away from Ben.

"What the hell was that?" he asks.

"That was your friend saving your ass, Sal," Nicky says. "He gave my mother an out and she took it, whether she really believes it or not. Now she'll go home to the 21-year-old Dominican pool boy she's been banging since you left."

Sal turns from Ben—who is now laughing hysterically—to Nicky.

"Wait a minute," he says. "If she's got a new toy, why does she care about me?"

"She doesn't. Or at least she didn't until I told her I found you. I'm the one who cares, and I need to put this 'misunderstanding' of yours behind us."

"Why?" Sal asks suspiciously.

"Because I want you to come home," Nicky says, finally removing his dark glasses to reveal big brown eyes. Ben winks at him and walks away.

"Again," Sal says. "Why?"

"You were one of my best earners, and you're not even part of my Family. Don't waste your time in this hick town. Come home."

"I like this town," Sal replies. "And I am home."

"Seriously?"

"Seriously. Plus, they rarely toss you in prison for selling books."

Nicky shakes his head sadly.

"That's a shame," he says. "But I had to at least ask."

"That's it?" Sal replies. "You come all the way down here, then no threats, no offers of big payoffs, nothing?"

"I don't threaten, I don't promise, and I don't beg," Nicky says flatly. "You say you're done, then you're done. But if I ever hear any different—"

"Right," Sal says. He has closed a door that cannot easily, or painlessly, be reopened. "Take care of yourself, Nicky." This time, they shake hands.

"One more thing," Nicky says. "I've been seeing this Russian dancer who likes to read and I thought I might give her something by Stroganoff or Yastrzemski or somebody like that."

"Turgenev or Dostoyevsky?" Sal corrects him.

"Whatever," Nicky says. "It just needs to be expensive. You got a rare book room in this place?"

"Not quite yet," he says, motioning for Jacob to join them. "But I think we can help you out anyway."

25

"A Mystery Solved"

Sal is in his room very early Saturday morning watching the videos he found in the apartment the first night, trying his best not to watch his aged uncle in various sexual positions. His search for his uncle's books has been futile thus far, but an idea came to him tonight that the tapes might tell him something. Not about Frank's prowess, of course. He is looking for something else entirely. He finds it, makes a note on a slip of paper, and walks out to the living room.

Camden is watching Arsenal vs. Tottenham Hotspur on the Fox Soccer Channel, the time difference allowing her to see the match before the store opens. She is perched on the edge of her stolen Emirates Stadium seat, screaming at the Arsenal manager.

"Wenger, you are a complete and total git!"

Sal sits down next to her.

"Wow," he says, "something actually does get you riled up besides me."

"Quiet," she says. "We're in stoppage time."

"I need to show you something."

"Wait."

"But—"

"Silence!"

He waits, having no clue what the hell stoppage time is. He can see that Arsenal is ahead 2-1, at least until a Tottenham player named Jenas fires a very nice shot from long range into the corner of the Arsenal goal. The whistle blows and Camden curses the television for several minutes. She then kisses the Arsenal scarf she's been wearing and gently folds it. He assumes there is no overtime in soccer, but does not ask.

"You done yet?"

"I suppose," she snaps. "What do you need?"

"I've been watching the tapes Uncle Frank made."

"Ick! For God's sake, why?"

"I'm looking for the books."

"The books?"

"Yeah. The ones you noticed were missing the first night here. Remember I said his library was the store?"

"Vaguely."

"I was wrong. Jacob said he had a good collection. Even put personalized bookplates in each book. Scott the

Book Scout found one of them; it was in that load he brought in the day we went to the thrift stores."

"Say that again," Camden says.

"Which part?"

"The part about you being wrong."

"Fine," he says. "I was wrong. Now focus."

"Right, the books. But what does the fact that Jacob said Frank had a collection have to do with the tapes?"

"The way the tripod was set up, you can see a bookcase in the far left of the picture."

"And?"

"And Frank could also have been nicknamed 'tripod,' for one thing. Dude was seriously hung. I see why so many of the Sirens—"

"Shut your face!" Camden screams, covering her ears. "I'm scarred just hearing that!"

"Ah, okay. Anyway, I figured out that the books were here when the last tape was made. There's no tape of the final...um...therapy session, so I can't pin it down exactly. But they were here a few months before he died. Then we get here and they're gone."

"Gone where? A book collection doesn't just disappear."

"No it does not. I'll talk to the Sirens tomorrow."

Camden is silent for a moment.

"You may want to ask the questions without mentioning the tapes, and definitely not that you saw them."

"Good point," he concedes.

A few days later, Sal is standing in front of the shop smoking. Heather walks down the sidewalk toward him carrying a small paper bag. She walks directly to him and pulls a book from the bag.

"Look at this," she says, thrusting the book into his hand.

Sal takes it and stares at it in wonder.

"Wow," he says, "it's a book."

"Yes, it's a book, smartass. Look more closely."

Sal examines the book. It is a first edition of a novel from the 1960s, not extremely valuable but in mint condition. The dust jacket is pristine, protected by a clear Mylar archival cover.

"It's a first edition in great shape, but it's no early Faulkner or Fitzgerald," he says.

"Look at the front endpaper."

He opens the book again and sees what he missed the first time. A bookplate is affixed to the front endpaper. It has an odd crest and bears the words "Ex Libris, Franklin Templeton."

"Where did you get this?"

"Crain Rare Books," she says. "I like to check out the competition, and I saw the bookplate when I flipped through this one, so I bought it."

"Randal's store? Were there others?"

"I didn't have time to look for more. Want me to go back and check?"

"Definitely."

Most of the staff has gathered on the rooftop bar after closing time at the shop that night, but not for relaxation. They are discussing Franklin's missing books.

"I just can't imagine how Randal could have gotten those books," Jacob says.

"Well, he obviously didn't steal them, right?" Julia asks. "Mr. Templeton would have reported them stolen if that had happened."

"Unless Frank was already gone," Sal replies. "When he died, did you close the shop for any length of time?"

"Yes," she says. "We closed for the normal three-day period. Actually, it may have been four. Then we reopened the day you got here. You don't think—"

"I think that's plenty of time for someone to steal the books," Sal says. "Trust me, an empty house is an easy house."

"Look, I hate that little shit Crain more than any of you," Jacob says. "But it makes no sense. There are plenty of books in the store worth a lot more than the ones in Frank's collection."

"Taking books from the store would have been noticed," Camden says. "As chaotic as his recordkeeping was, there was still inventory, invoices, tracking mechanisms. You would have caught it immediately. But who knew what was in his personal collection? Even Sal didn't give it much thought."

"But what can we do about it?" Julia asks. "And are we sure the one you found wasn't just a fluke?"

"Heather counted at least seventy books in Crain's store with Uncle Frank's bookplate in them," Sal says.

"Closer to ninety," Heather corrects him.

"Right. So there's plenty of evidence."

"Then we should call the police," Camden says confidently.

"Won't work," Jacob says. "Crain will simply say Frank sold them to him in a dealer-to-dealer transaction. Lots of those happen, in cash, with no paper trail. It's his word against our suspicions."

"Then I'll go see him myself," Sal says. "We already know he's afraid of me; maybe I can spook him into admitting it."

Julia and Camden both give him a disapproving look.

"And get yourself arrested in the process," Julia says. "How would it look if the master thief got pinched shaking down a bookseller? You'd never live it down."

"Yes, you have a reputation to consider," Camden says. "I think I should go. I can reason with people."

"Right," Sal says mockingly. "We've all seen that. Your powers of persuasion are amazing, as long as a six-foot-four Puerto Rican mountain shows up to save the day. Ortiz won't be there to help you this time."

"But—"

"No," he says. "I'm doing this. And the less you all know beforehand, the better. Give me two hours...and stay here. I may need an alibi."

He gets up and leaves the bar as the group watches helplessly.

Randal Crain stands in the master bathroom of his house, brushing his teeth. He wears plaid pajamas that are a size too large. He rinses, turns off the bathroom light, and enters the bedroom. As his eyes fall on a chair in the corner he nearly screams. Sal is sitting in the chair, reading the book that Heather first showed him. His pistol rests comfortably in his right hand.

"What the hell are you doing in my house?!" he screams after recovering from his initial shock.

"Calm down, Randy. We have something to discuss that simply can't wait until morning."

"How did you get in here?"

"You have a substandard alarm system and locks that wouldn't deter a pre-schooler, but that's not important right now."

"I'm calling the police," Randal says.

"You have no home phone, and your cell is in my pocket, so that would be a neat trick. Go ahead."

Crain turns a deep red, either from anger or embarrassment or both.

"Get out!"

"Not just yet," Sal says calmly. "How about you tell me why my uncle's book collection is for sale in your store."

He flips open the book to show Crain the bookplate. Crain sits down on the edge of the bed, clearly surprised at this turn in the conversation.

"I bought them from him," Crain says, "not long before he died, actually."

"You're gonna have to do better than that, Randy." Sal puts the book down and raises the gun. "Hmmm...should I start with the left knee or the right?"

Crain's demeanor shifts immediately from angry to terrified.

"I swear Franklin sold them to me," he says quickly. "I have the bill of sale with his signature, and I can get a copy of the check I wrote him. Please, God, don't shoot me."

"Why would he sell you his collection? And why would you want it? There aren't any mega-dollar books in there."

"He said he needed the money or the store would close," Randal says, talking so fast Sal can barely understand him. "He couldn't sell me any of the store's stock because he still needed that, plus he didn't want Weinberg to know. He couldn't even meet payroll that month. He said he couldn't let his employees down, that they were his family."

Sal lowers the gun, but not completely.

"So out of the kindness of your heart you bailed out a competitor? Horseshit."

"Hey, booksellers share a bond," Crain protested. "I felt compassion for his staff. It was the right thing to do."

"Are you hoping one of those three lies will make me all weepy?"

"Fine, I got them cheap."

"Now we're getting somewhere. Still, he sold a collection he spent his whole life assembling, hundreds and hundreds of books, just to save a few people's jobs?"

"Admirable, you have to admit. I'd never have done that myself, but still very admirable."

"Very," Sal says. "So where is this receipt? And if you cheated my elderly uncle in his time of need, I'm going to hurt you. Badly."

Sal is recounting the conversation with Crain to the group at the table. He does not show them the copy of the receipt Crain gave him. There is no need.

"I can't believe he did that for us," Julia says.

"Sentimental old fool," Jacob says.

"So how long before the cops come for you?" Camden asks Sal.

"No cops. He's not even going to call them."

"Why in the world not? I certainly would if you broke into my house."

"He says it's because he understands that I was upset, thinking he'd robbed my uncle right after he died. I think it's because he saw how easily I can get into his house and the fact that I have a table full of people who will swear under oath that I was here the whole night."

"You're mental," Cam says. "I wouldn't swear to that, not under oath at least. It would be a lie."

"Me neither," Heather agrees.

"Sorry," Julia says. "Not me either. Perjury gets jail time, and I'm too cute to go to the slammer."

"I would," Jacob says finally.

Everyone turns to him, surprised.

"I'd perjure myself to the Supreme Court if it meant getting over on that weasel Crain," Jacob says. "I just wish I could have been there to see his face when he found you in his room. Priceless."

From the street below, a horn sounds: three short beeps and one long one. Camden gets up from the table.

"That's my date," Camden says brightly. "Sal, be a peach and pay my tab; consider it the price for my testimony."

She goes down the stairs, and all of them rush to the roof's edge to see who her date is. As she comes out the door on street level, a huge Latin man exits a new Cadillac SUV and opens the passenger door for her. He looks up to the roof and waves, then gets back in the car and roars away.

"Who was that gorgeous creature?" Heather asks.

"That was Ramon's uncle, Luis," Julia says with a sigh.

Sal gives her a sharp look. She simply shrugs and walks back to the table.

It is well after 3 am when Camden returns to the apartment, where she is surprised to find Sal awake and watching television in the living room.

"Waiting up for me?" she asks. "How sweet."

"Don't flatter yourself," he replies, clearly having trouble keeping his eyes open. "*The Godfather* is on."

"So? You have it on DVD."

"Doesn't matter," he says. "If you're channel surfing and stumble across *The Godfather*, you cannot turn it off or change the channel. You have to watch it; it's a rule."

"A rule?" she asks, incredulous. "Whose rule?"

"It's a guy rule," he says, becoming a little more alert. "You wouldn't understand."

"Is this an Italian guy rule?"

"Nope, ask any guy. Italian, Irish, white, black, Hispanic, straight, gay… I bet even your ex-husband knows the rule."

"Is this true for any other film?" she asks.

"*The Godfather, Part II* is the only other."

"Ah," she says, clearly thinking this is a stupid rule. "So do you want to know how my date went?"

"Well, to be honest I am a little curious," Sal replies. "Ortiz isn't exactly the type I figured you'd go for."

She plops down next to him on the couch and grabs his arm, her excitement overpowering the sounds of Carlo Rizzi being garroted on the television. *Great,* Sal thinks, *now we're girlfriends.*

"He's not my type *at all*," she replies in a near-squeal. "That's what I like so much about him. He's just so, so, *not* English."

Sal removes her hand, stands up, and walks to the fridge for a beer. This is going to take a while.

"What exactly does 'not English' mean?" he asks. "Besides the obvious fact that he's not English." She grabs the beer from his hand and takes a swig. He returns to the fridge for another.

"It means not English," she repeats. "I know that Americans have this vision of English men being either dashing, like James Bond, or sweet and sensitive, like those characters Hugh Grant always plays—"

"You mean they're not?" Sal interrupts sarcastically. "I'm shocked."

"I'm serious," she says. Sal thinks Cam may be a little drunk. "They're not like that at all, at least none of the ones I ever knew. A date to them is watching football or cricket on the telly in a pub, with a cheese and pickle sandwich with crisps at the half serving as a romantic dinner."

"Remind me again," Sal says. "What you call crisps are what we call chips, and what you call chips we call fries, right?"

"For the millionth time, yes," she says with an exasperated sigh. "Pay attention. Actually, that sums up English men quite well: they simply don't pay attention to you when you're dating, except when they want sex, and sometimes not even then. I think I fell for Giles because he was attentive early on, which should have been the first sign that he was gay. He also paid the entire bill at dinner, even after I ordered dessert."

"So English guys force girls to watch sports, avoid fancy restaurants, and ignore you except when they want to get laid. Sounds a lot like Jersey to me."

"But it's not," she insists, her voice rising. She leaps up, sloshing beer from the bottle onto the floor; now he knows she's drunk. "It's not the same at all. Well, I've actually only been to New Jersey that one time for Silvio's funeral and I was only nine but I can't believe it's any different there than what I've experienced here, where men will actually walk straight up to me in the store, customers no less, and ask if I'd like to have dinner with them or go away for the weekend to their lake house or to a comedy club but never, ever to watch Wigan play Leicester City in the 3rd round of the FA Cup at the Pig and Whistle, and they almost always have their own car and never live with their mum."

She stops to take a breath and Sal takes advantage of the pause.

"That was one long sentence, Miss Bennet," he says. She stares at him for a second, then snorts with laughter.

"I get that!" she exclaims. "Elizabeth Bennet…a Jane Austen reference. Bet you thought I wouldn't catch it, Mr. I Know Everything About Books Including What a Point Is. Ha! Every English girl knows Jane. Jane's part of the problem, filling our heads from the time we can walk with the fool notion that there's a Mr. Darcy out there waiting for us if we will only persevere and not settle for Mr. Close Enough just because he's about to be named Vicar of the local parish and our mums are afraid we'll end up like Miss Havisham if we don't."

"Stop," Sal says, holding up his hand. She does, a quizzical look on her face. "Breathe." She does, then picks up where she left off.

"Don't misunderstand," she says. "Most English guys are very well mannered, and most of them dress better than the average American man, but they're just so stiff and awkward. They're great with dogs—that's one stereotype that really is true. I wish they were as good with women as they are with dogs. But here it's different. Luis and I talked, actually talked, for hours tonight. We talked about everything and anything. And I could tell he wasn't just listening to what I had to say hoping to get me into the sack."

"How could you tell that?" Sal asks.

"Because he told me when he picked me up at the Dream Emporium that no matter how much he might want to, and no matter how much I tried to persuade him, we were not having intimate knowledge of each other on our first date. His exact words, more or less. And he opened doors for me and pulled out the chair and stood up when I got up to go to the loo. He's like a Puerto Rican Mr. Darcy."

"Good lord," Sal says, rolling his eyes. "You are drunk. And apparently easily impressed by what is really nothing more that normal human interaction. How in God's name did you people rule half the globe for so long?"

"Don't change the subject," she says, slurring her words a little. "And Luis is American, because Puerto Rico is part of America. He doesn't think so, but I looked it up."

"You looked it up? Amazing."

"I thought so too," she says with a wobbly nod. "All this time I thought Puerto Rico was its own country. Luis claims it's actually a kingdom with a throne to which he is the legitimate heir, and that the territory stolen from his kingdom over the years includes Cuba, Florida, Venezuela, and the Bronx."

"Hard to argue against any of those," Sal concedes. "Look, Cam, I like Ortiz personally, and I admire anyone who manages to live life according to his own rules. But surely even in your inebriated state you can see that he is more than a little insane."

"He's colorful," she replies defensively. "And he speaks very highly of you, unlike most people. I suppose there really is honor among thieves." She laughs so hard at her own joke that she falls off the couch. Sal stands and helps her up.

"Time for bed, cousin," he says, taking the beer from her and steering her toward her bedroom door, which is no simple task given her state. "We can discuss all of this in a few hours when you're sober and I've had some sleep."

As he closes her bedroom door, Sal is grateful that he'll get at least a couple hours of shut-eye before the alarm goes off. Then he glances at the television; *The Godfather, Part II* has started. Apparently they're showing both back-to-back.

"Damn it," he says softly, then walks to the kitchen to make more coffee.

26

"A Secret Revealed"

It is 2 am Saturday morning and Camden is riding in Heather's car, returning from yet another showing of *The Rocky Horror Picture Show*. The ancient Mazda careens through the streets of downtown, Heather talking non-stop and paying little attention to the mostly deserted streets. Camden has gotten used to driving on the right side of the road, but regardless, Heather's reckless driving makes her a tad uncomfortable.

"The crowd seemed a little sparse tonight," Heather says.

"There's a comic book convention in town," Camden replies. "I think a lot of the regulars went there instead. Geeks."

"I've been thinking that we should get the whole staff to go with us one night," Heather says, taking a turn much too fast for Camden's comfort. "In costume, of course. Julia would make the perfect Janet."

Camden laughs at this, momentarily forgetting the fact that they could be killed at any moment. This gives her a thought as well.

"I rather fancy the idea of Sal having to dress as Dr. Frank-N-Furter," she says with a giggle.

"No," Heather replies. "Jacob can be Frank-N-Furter. I want to see Sal in nothing but Rocky's gold shorts. Can't tell you how many times I almost whispered 'touch-a touch-a touch me' to him when we've been alone in the store."

"Good lord!" Camden says. "That's my cousin you're talking about, remember?"

"He makes me want to be dirty," Heather says in a raspy voice; they both laugh at this. "That jackass Randal would make a good Frank-N-Furter too."

"Actually, my ex-husband Giles would likely make the best transvestite of the lot," Camden muses. "Probably already has the entire costume hanging in what used to be my bloody closet. The tosser."

"What's a tosser?" Heather asks, turning to her.

Camden is about to explain when she realizes that Heather is not slowing for a red light as they approach the intersection of Throckmorton Street and Second Street.

"Stop!" she screams, pointing toward the stoplight.

Heather slams on the brakes and they screech to a stop, tires smoking. She looks back at Camden with an apologetic smile, then makes an exaggerated effort to focus on the road ahead of her.

Just before the light changes, a crowd spills out of a bar across the street; it is closing time and the diehard revelers are being shown the door. Camden does a double-take when she sees who she thinks are Sal and Julia walk out, hand-in-hand. The light changes. As the car draws even with the couple, the man—who is definitely Sal—leans down and kisses the woman, who is most certainly Julia. In a moment the car is past them.

"Did you see that?" Camden asks Heather.

"See what?"

Camden pauses briefly, straining to see the couple in the car's side mirror.

"Nothing," she says finally.

The car rolls down the deserted street toward Cam's apartment. She is quite confident Sal will not be home, and she smiles to herself at the thought.

Later that same Saturday morning, Camden and Sal are walking back from Kate's Bakery. Camden carries a box of donuts and Sal carries several coffees in a Styrofoam carrier. He tries to smoke at the same time, with both hands full, and is having difficulty.

"You should give up that filthy habit," Camden says.

"What do you care?" The cigarette bobs up and down as he speaks. "I don't smoke in the apartment or the store, even if it's raining, and if I get lung cancer you'll own everything."

"Actually, I think your half would go to your relatives. I mean, like your mum or sisters."

"Nope," he says casually. "It all goes to you. I changed my will last month."

She is shocked.

"Sal..."

"Not a word, Limey. It doesn't mean my heart isn't cold and black. I just dislike you a tad less than the rest of my family. I totally understand Franklin's attitude about this."

"From what I saw last night, I would think you might be adding another person to the list of those you don't dislike," she says.

"What the hell does that mean?" Sal asks, trying to inhale smoke while talking.

"Oh, nothing."

Sal stops and puts the coffee carrier on the ground so he can toss his cigarette into the gutter.

"What exactly did you see, cousin?"

She doesn't answer at once, enjoying the fact that this is bothering him. He makes no move to pick up the coffee.

"Well, coming home from Rocky Horror the other night I saw a couple that looked a lot like a cousin of mine and my best employee...snogging."

"Snogging?"

"Yes," she says. "You know, kissing."

"I know what snogging means, Cam. I've seen the Harry Potter movies."

"Ah, quite."

"Ah, quite?" he repeats.

"Are you just going to repeat everything I say, or are you going to admit that you and Julia are seeing each other?"

"I admit nothing," he replies. "At least not until I check with her, hypothetically speaking."

"Ha! I knew it. I knew it from the first day when I said she was smitten with you."

"Everyone gets to be right once in a while."

He picks up the coffee carrier and begins walking again. Camden hurries to catch up to him.

"Wait!" she exclaims. "You can't just leave it at that. Tell me what's going on."

"No. I am not giving you the details of my private life so you can sit around with Heather and the Sirens and stir up trouble."

"Stir up trouble?!"

"Now you're repeating what I say."

"You're the one stirring up trouble. I can't believe you would take advantage of that young girl just because she foolishly appears to be in love with you."

"It's not like that," he says sharply. They are nearing the store, and he is not slowing down.

"Stop! I don't want to talk about this inside the shop."

He stops and turns to face her. His expression is not angry, but nor is it friendly.

"I don't either, so let's not, okay?"

"What do you mean it's not like that?" Camden asks.

He sets down the coffee again and lights another cigarette. He takes several drags in silence, then realizes Camden is not going to let this go.

"It means she's not the only one who's smitten," he says. "And that's all you're getting out of me, Sherlock." He flicks the barely-smoked cigarette into the street, picks up the coffee, and walks into the bookstore. Camden doesn't move for a moment, then she smiles broadly and follows him inside.

The store has not opened yet. Sal hands cups of coffee to the staff working that morning as Camden sets the box of donuts on the counter. Everyone grabs one except Jacob, who instead scoops up all of the donut holes scattered throughout the box and flees before anyone can protest. After Sal takes a large bite from a chocolate éclair,

Julia uses her napkin to wipe some chocolate from the corner of his mouth. Only Camden notices.

27

"Just When I Thought It Was Safe To Go Back In The Store"

There is a crowd in the store a few weeks later, following a reading and signing by a local author. Everyone is in an upbeat mood. After the last customer and the guest author depart, Camden gathers the staff around the checkout counter. Sal sits on the back counter flipping through a stack of mail.

"I just want to thank everyone for making tonight such a success, especially Julia for finding the author in the first place."

There are claps and whistles. Julia makes a theatrical bow.

"I also want to let you know," Camden continues, "that for the first time since we took over this store, and maybe for the first time in a long time, our month-end numbers show a significant profit. We're in the black!"

There are considerably louder claps and whistles, along with a collective sigh of relief. Ramon starts singing

AC/DC's *Back in Black*. Sal, however, is intently reading a letter he has just opened.

"And although there is still a lot of work to do to get where we want to be," she concludes, "I think the changes everyone has helped make will keep us moving in the right direction."

Before more cheers can begin, Sal punctures the festive mood.

"Well fuck me!" he exclaims. The room goes silent and every head turns toward him.

"What?" Camden asks, spinning around to face him. "What's wrong?"

"What's wrong is that our little celebration is apparently premature," he says.

He hands her the letter. She reads it quickly, gives him a horrified look, then reads it again. She leans in close to him and whispers.

"I think we should discuss this privately."

"I disagree," he says with a shake of his head. "Everyone here has a stake in this place. We've been totally up front with them to this point...no sense stopping now."

He takes the letter back and walks around to the front of the counter. He looks at each member of his staff, his friends, before speaking.

"Though Franklin had been in this building for decades, it seems he never actually bought it; probably never could afford to. But the rent has been amazingly low, which helped a lot as we were turning things around. According to this letter, the building was sold to a commercial developer recently, and the deal closed last week."

"So we have a new landlord?" Jacob asks. "Does that mean the rent goes up?"

"Yes," Sal replies, "we have a new landlord. But no, the rent isn't going up. The new owner plans on tearing down the building and putting up a parking garage in its place. We're being evicted."

No one speaks. They simply stare at Sal, dumbfounded.

"There has to be some way to stop it, right?" Julia finally asks. "It's an historic building after all. He can't just tear it down."

"Not historic enough," Sal says. "We found that out when we applied for the permits to renovate the outside. If it was five years older we wouldn't have been able to make those changes, and this guy wouldn't be able to tear it down either. But it's not five years older."

Ramon steps up and strikes a defiant pose.

"Maybe we could barricade the place and hold him off for the next five years," he says.

Sal smiles at his youthful idealism, but shakes his head.

"I wish, Ramon. But we don't have the firepower for that. And we don't have five years. We have thirty days to vacate the place."

At this point everyone begins speaking at once.

"I'll call Billings first thing in the morning," Camden says. "We'll sue to stop this travesty."

"This can't happen," Julia says. "Not after how hard we've worked to save this place."

"I am not going back to work at Target," Heather says.

"Arizona...with my sisters-in-law...I hate the desert," says Jacob. "This cannot be happening."

"My husband is going to expect me to get a real job," Siren One says. "Damn it."

"You're lucky," Siren Two tells her. "Mine will want to fire the maid and make me do the cleaning."

"This may be the spark that ignites *la revolucion*," Ramon says with a faraway look in his eyes.

"There's not another independent bookstore within 75 miles of here," Julia says. "Unless I ask Randal Crain for a job. And I'd rather eat broken glass than do that." She shudders at the thought.

"We'll lose our apartment, Sal," Camden says. "I didn't even think about that. No job and no home. I'll have to go back to England and move in with my mum." She shudders at that thought, too.

Sal does not speak for a long time. He simply studies the faces of these people who have become his family as their voices blend into one raucous sound. He has an obligation to them, and is suddenly angry. He slams his fist down on the counter, which silences the room.

"Everybody just calm down," he says, rubbing his hand. "We're not going to lose this bookstore, and Cam, we're not going to lose our home. I'm going to take care of everything."

The dumbfounded looks return, but are quickly replaced by hopeful expressions on every face except Julia's.

"What are you going to do, Sal?" she asks, suspiciously.

He gives her a reassuring smile.

"Trust me, angel. I'm gonna make the ass-hat an offer he can't refuse."

He ushers everyone out before they can ask him any more questions. Before Ramon exits, Sal puts a hand on his shoulder and whispers in his ear.

"I may need your Uncle Luis's phone number."

Early the next morning, Sal strides through the living room, dressed uncharacteristically in a black suit and white dress shirt. His black cowboy boots are shined to the point of gleaming. Camden sits at the table drinking coffee, and she is surprised by his outfit.

"Somebody die?" she asks.

"Huh?" Sal asks, distracted. He had not even noticed her sitting there.

"You look like you're dressed for a funeral. I didn't even know you owned a suit, just boots and jeans."

"Cute," he says, straightening his tie. "No, I'm going to see Mr. Ass-Hat about our building, and it never hurts to look professional."

He takes his wallet off the kitchen counter, and as he pushes his suit jacket back to put the wallet in his back pocket, Camden sees the gun in his waistband.

"No," she says firmly.

"No what?"

"No, you are not going over there with a gun, Sal. Absolutely not. Randal was one thing, but this is different. We'll find another way to solve this. Or we'll open in a new location."

"Right," he says with a mirthless laugh, "since we have so much cash just lying around. That would take more than even *I* can steal."

She doesn't even smile at the joke.

"Regardless," she says, "you are not going over there and threatening that man. All you'll accomplish is getting yourself arrested."

"I don't get arrested, kiddo. In fact, there are some very reputable gentlemen who will testify under oath that at this very moment I am 200 miles away, in a boat on Lake Travis, fishing."

Camden smacks herself on the forehead.

"You don't fish!"

"Of course I do. Why would the witnesses lie about something like that? And for your information, I always carry a gun. It's my birthright as an Italian-American."

"No."

"You said that already," he says. "You're repeating yourself again."

"Please, Sal."

"It will be fine, Cam," he says, walking to the door. "I'm just going to talk to him."

"Leave the gun then."

He opens the door.

"Can't do that."

"If you won't leave it for me," she pleads, "leave it for Julia."

He pauses in the open doorway, his back to her. He replies without turning to her.

"Julia, you, our friends downstairs...you're all the reason I can't leave it. I'm sorry."

He steps through the doorway and closes the door behind him. She doesn't try to follow him.

Twenty minutes later Sal sits in a comfortable leather wingback chair across an enormous desk from Robert Milner, a fit, tanned man in his early 60s, previously known as Mr. Ass-Hat, the real estate mogul who now owns their building. Sal had expected something different, more pompous or oily or even a little seedy, but Milner seems like just a regular guy. A regular guy who is throwing him and his friends out on the street.

"I understand this is difficult, Mr. Terranova..." he says.

"Call me Sal."

"I realize it's difficult, Sal, but I'm a businessman. Just like I've heard you are."

Sal arches an eyebrow, but lets the comment pass.

"It's more profitable for me to tear the place down and build a parking garage; people always need somewhere to park."

Sal still says nothing as Milner drones on. He slides his hand down to where he can feel the pistol through the material of his suit jacket. His fingers begin to slowly pull the jacket back. Then he notices the painting on the wall behind Milner's desk. It is modeled after Da Vinci's *Last Supper*, but with a twist: in place of Christ and the apostles are characters from Mafia films. At the center, where Jesus would be, is Marlon Brando as Don Vito Corleone. Flanking him on one side are Al Pacino, Robert Duvall, Joe Pesci, Paul Sorvino, and James Gandolfini. On the other side are Robert DeNiro, Ray Liotta, James Caan, Abe Vigoda, Richard Castellano, and John Cazale. He knows immediately who painted it.

"That's a very interesting painting," Sal says.

Milner swivels his chair around quickly and gazes at the painting. It is obvious that he is proud of it.

"Like it?" he asks. "Believe it or not it was painted by a guy in Federal Prison. I commissioned it myself. I paid for his latest appeal, actually."

He swivels back around to face Sal, who still has his hand near his gun. Milner's eyes have brightened.

"I collect what you might call Mob memorabilia," he says, all thoughts of real estate vanished. "It holds a fascination for me I can't really explain. That's the main reason I agreed to see you: your connection to that, um, life. No offense."

"None taken," Sal assures him. "So you knew who I was when I called."

"Yes, I did. Although I have to admit I was a little worried that you would be angry, and might come in here guns blazing. Overactive imagination."

"Yeah," Sal says with a laugh more genuine than uncomfortable. "That only happens in the movies. So what else do you have, in your collection I mean?"

Sal is simply making conversation to buy some time. He still hasn't completely decided on his course of action, but he knows he needs to make his move soon.

"Most of it is at my house," Milner says. "I have the original chair that Brando was sitting in at the start of *The Godfather*, the prop shotgun Pacino carried in the Sicily scenes from the same movie, and the car DeNiro drove in *Goodfellas*. A bunch more stuff like that."

Sal nods and gives this some thought.

"So all movie-related stuff, nothing connected to real gangsters."

"Sadly, no," Milner says, shaking his head." That stuff doesn't come on the market very often, and when it does it's out of my league."

"I would think a real estate tycoon could afford anything," Sal says.

"Hell, son, I'm not even a tycoon in Fort Worth," he says with a snort. "Medium-sized fish in a medium-sized pond."

Milner spins back around to admire the painting again, his back completely to Sal now. Sal takes advantage of this and slides his jacket all the way back so he can reach his gun.

"What I wouldn't give to have a real Mafia treasure in my collection," Milner says, still not turning around.

Sal pauses, grips the butt of his gun, and stands.

28

"If My Mother Needed a Heart Transplant"

A gloomy group of people assemble for work that day. Julia is on the phone, Jacob forlornly organizing Russian authors, Ramon helping him. Camden is furiously working a calculator and scribbling numbers. Even Siren One isn't herself, showing little interest in the job she is doing polishing her nails. The door opens and Sal walks in. Everyone stares at him.

"Jesus," he says, "what a morose group you are."

Julia hangs up the phone and Camden slams down her pencil.

"Where the hell have you been for two days?" she demands. "We've been worried sick." She glances at Julia. "I mean, I've been worried sick. You never even called."

"Sorry, mum. I didn't realize I had a curfew."

"Don't be a wiseguy," she says.

He arches an eyebrow at her and smiles.

"Right. Poor choice of words. Where were you?"

"Out. I had some things to take care of."

"For two days?" Julia asks, a note of derision in her tone.

"Yes, boss. But it was worth it. I got this." He pulls an envelope from his back pocket and hands it to Camden. She opens it and removes a folded piece of paper, reads it, then looks at Sal, wide-eyed.

"How?" she asks.

"How what?" Jacob asks. "What is it?"

Camden is still looking at Sal, weighing the multiple ramifications of this in her mind.

"It's the deed to our building," she answers. "In Sal's name."

"We can add yours later," he says. "I don't think it's a difficult procedure."

Everyone has gathered around her to look at the deed, not grasping how this miracle could have happened. But Camden thinks she knows, as does Julia.

"Answer her question, Sal," Julia says coldly. "How did you get it?"

"I made him an offer he couldn't refuse," he replies with a wink.

"No more jokes. How?"

Everyone is staring at them now, but neither seem to notice. It is as if they are alone in the store, caught in a Mexican standoff.

"If you must know, it turns out the gentleman is quite the fan of all things Mafia. Big collector of Mob movie memorabilia. Wow, that's not easy to say."

"So?"

"So, he only has movie-related stuff."

"And?" Julia says, a little less coldly.

"And would you believe that in his whole collection he had nothing that personally belonged to Lucky Luciano, the greatest gangster of all time?"

Julia's expression changes immediately. Though Camden doesn't know about the book, she senses from Julia's reaction that Sal did not, in fact, shoot the man. Julia starts to cry.

"Oh, Sally..." she says, her voice breaking.

"I mean, think about it," he continues. "A Mob fan not having something owned by Lucky is like a baseball aficionado owning nothing of Babe Ruth's. It's just not right."

Julia is no longer listening. She walks straight up to him, throws her arms around his neck, and buries her face in his chest.

"Okay," Sal says, "so maybe Babe Ruth isn't the best example. You like Ted Williams better?"

"Shut up, you big goombah."

He does. She doesn't release him, so he simply wraps his arms around her and rocks her back and forth. Everyone is still staring.

"What the heck is going on?" Jacob asks. "What did all that mean?"

"It means we're back in business," Sal says. "Go sell some books."

No one moves. Julia looks up into his eyes, then kisses him.

There are smiles and nods and the group disperses. Jacob mutters and hands a twenty-dollar bill to Ramon. Camden walks up to them; Julia will not let go of him.

"I suppose at some point you're going to explain to your business partner what your girlfriend already seems to know."

Before he can respond, Julia releases him and turns to Camden.

"There's nothing to explain, Cam. He was in Atlantic City the whole time."

"Actually," he replies, "I was fishing on Lake Travis."

"Whatever," Julia says, and kisses him again.

29

"Full Circle"

The bookshop is crowded with customers for a signing event by two new local authors. A pyramid of copies of their new book dominates the center of the store. The title is *Bolivar, Guevara, and Beyond: A New Manifesto for Our Oppressed Latin Brothers*. Only the authors' first names appear on the book: Ramon and Luis.

Everyone, it seems, has shown up for this momentous occasion. Kate has provided cupcakes, and Eddie Donovan sent two cases of wine ("and not the cheap stuff, either"). Scott the Book Scout is getting several books signed by both Luis and Ramon, obviously in the hope that they will someday be famous and he the owner of some very valuable first editions.

Jake Donovan is there with a very tall, very attractive blonde woman. Heather, who has had her eye on Jake since he entered the store, watches as they appear to have a significant disagreement about something. The woman walks to the religion section, while Jake heads for Fiction.

Heather moves that direction herself. As she approaches him, Jake is looking at a copy of Maugham's *The Razor's Edge.*

"Can I help you find anything?" she asks him.

"No," he says, looking up from the book. His gaze lingers on her for a long moment, longer than he realizes, which she takes as a good sign. "Just looking. This is actually one of my favorite books. I read it once a year."

She takes the book from him and reads the back cover, then hands it back.

"I've never read that one," she admits. "I'm more of a Lost Generation fan myself, but I'm open to new things."

She gives him a blatantly wicked smile as she says this, even licking her lips at the end, yet he does not seem shocked in the least. If this is the guy Camden told her about, apparently his mobster/sniper side is stronger than his preacher side.

"I like a woman with an open mind," he says, holding her gaze for so long she finally has to look away.

"Then you should read Hemingway to me sometime," she says, looking up again.

"I'm Jake, by the way."

"I know," she answers. "Camden told us about you and the thing with Ramon's principal. I'm Heather."

Before he can say anything else, his blonde Amazon companion walks up to them. She completely ignores Heather.

"Jake, they have a whole shelf of Buddhist books in the religion section," she says, indignant. "Can you imagine? Books on Eastern cults sitting next to the Bibles."

"It's the religion section, Amy," he says. "Buddhism is a religion."

"It's Satanic," she replies. "And I do not understand why you're not as outraged as I am."

"You have obviously forgotten that not every bookstore is like the one inside your father's church or on the Baylor campus."

"Well, the world would be a much better place if they were. How long do we have to stay?"

"Not much longer," he says with a heavy sigh. "I just need to say goodbye to Lou."

"All right," she says, pleased that this foray to the dark side will soon be over. "I'm going to grab one of those cupcakes." She walks to a table where Kate has set up her goodies, leaving Jake alone with Heather again.

"Sorry about that," he says. "She's not usually...ah hell, yeah, she usually is."

Heather laughs out loud, and Jake smiles broadly. She has a great laugh.

"I guess I need to get going," he continues, "but it was nice meeting you. Maybe I'll see you again the next time I'm here."

"Nice meeting you too," she says. "And definitely come back soon. We can discuss books, and open minds."

She holds out her hand, which he takes. Looking into her eyes, he holds it a fraction longer than politeness dictates. *A very good sign*, she thinks as he walks away.

Camden is chatting with Kate when she notices Siren One arm-in-arm with Ben, the unfortunately gay Greek god of the sci-fi section. She excuses herself, then pulls Siren One aside.

"Andrea," she whispers, "what in the world are you doing?" Unlike Sal, she actually uses the Sirens' real names.

"I told you I could turn him," she says proudly. "Actually, I didn't completely turn him; more like a half-turn. He's my very own Mickey Mantle."

"Who?" Camden asks, confused.

"Sorry," Andrea says. "I forget sometimes that you're not from here. Mickey Mantle was the greatest switch hitter in baseball history. Like the Mick, Big Ben now hits from both sides of the plate." She winks at Camden and goes back to Ben's side.

Ortiz has just finished a very dramatic reading from the first chapter of his book, to thunderous applause. He walks over to where Sal is leaning against the wall, stopping to sign a few books along the way.

"A fine turn-out for a groundbreaking event, my friend," he says.

"Definitely. And your reading was a hit."

"That's no surprise," Ortiz says. "The men of my country are as gifted at oratory as they are at romance. Surely you knew this, being a man of the world."

"It must have slipped my mind."

Ortiz nods, then looks around the store until he catches sight of Ramon. His nephew is surrounded by teenage girls in berets and Che Guevara shirts, basking in the attention. Ortiz smiles.

"I cannot express my gratitude to you and the lovely Camden for publishing our manifesto," he says. "It means a great deal to Ramon. You have both been extremely good friends to him, and I will not forget it."

"Don't mention it," Sal says. "I wish there were more kids out there like him...and less like us." They both laugh.

"I have a gift for you in any case, just to say thank you. I have one for the lovely Camden as well, but it is not for public viewing."

He hands Sal a small package. It is wrapped in colorful paper adorned with cartoon penguins and the words

"Happy Birthday." Sal gives him a puzzled look, and stares suspiciously at the animated penguins.

"It was the only wrapping paper the store had," Ortiz explains.

"I see."

"I know of your aversion to penguins," Ortiz says, "because of the holy sisters. Ramon mentioned it when I bought the paper. But it is appropriate to the occasion. Penguins are very manly. Emperor Penguins...kings of birds."

"Of course."

Sal unwraps the package just as Julia walks over to them. As he reveals what's inside, Julia gasps.

"Where did you get that?" she asks, clearly shocked.

Sal stares down, not believing what he sees. He looks up at Ortiz.

"From Luis," he says, his voice barely above a whisper. "Lou, how in the world did you get this?"

Ortiz makes a dismissive motion with his hand.

"Child's play," he says. "You told the lovely Camden how you saved the store—and my nephew's job, by the way. The lovely Camden told me one night at dinner. And voila, the book of Luciano has returned home."

Sal turns the book over in his hands, and Julia puts her hand on his shoulder.

"Luis, how did you—" she says.

He interrupts her.

"I did nothing, dear Julia. As fate would have it, I was in San Juan the entire night. There is a nightclub full of witnesses and a properly stamped passport that says so."

30

"Paris Stays With You"

The antique street lamps along Houston Street cast an eerie glow filtered through the rain that arrived after closing time, thumping against the tinted-glass display windows at the front of the shop. The light, however, illuminates nothing and the rain drenches no one; the streets are empty. Inside the shop, Sal leans back against the front checkout counter. The receiver of an ancient rotary phone rests on his shoulder, an unlit cigarette dangling absently from his lips.

"Yes, sir," he says into the phone, "I'm quite familiar with the book. It is, after all, a classic." He pauses while the person on the other end of the phone speaks.

"Yes, I understand that we say we can find any book for any customer." The store motto is etched in the glass of the front window, after all. There is another long pause.

"Yes, sir, if you are willing to pay the price it's typically not that difficult to find a signed Hemingway." There's a longer pause while the caller speaks more loudly.

"Again, I'm sorry to say there simply are no signed copies of *A Moveable Feast* available anywhere." This time the pause is much shorter.

"Because it was published three years after Hemingway died." Long pause.

"Yes, sir, I'm quite certain." After yet another pause, Sal gently places the telephone receiver back in its cradle. The caller has hung up.

Sal laughs out loud in the empty store as he turns to watch the rain outside grow heavier. A signed copy of *A Moveable Feast*. It was a crazy request, of course, but then he had seen more than a few crazy things since he went from burglar to bookseller.

Acknowledgements

It is impossible to thank every person who played a part in the creation of this novel; the list covers the spectrum from Starbucks baristas to public librarians to the E Street Band. But those listed below played crucial roles in bringing the novel to life:

The following were Goodfellas-level or higher contributors to the Pubslush crowdfunding campaign that got things off the ground: Chris Davis, Philip Sams, Steven Mentzel, Don and Ellen Stevenson, Donnie and Catharine Nunn, Shannon Barnes, Marilyn Rising, and Beth Saladino. Thanks to all of you, and to everyone who supported the project at any level.

Thanks to Michelle Josette, who edited the final manuscript into shape. You are a much better Max Perkins than I'll ever be a Hemingway.

Thanks to my sister, Indi Butler...as always, for everything. Tramps like us, and all that.

Once again, all my love to my daughters, who get mentioned in both the front and the back of this book. That's more than you expected and less than you deserve.

Paul Combs is a writer living in the not always literary state of Texas. His ultimate goal (besides being a roadie for the E Street Band) is to make reading, writing, and books in general as popular in Texas as high school football. It may take a while.

The Last Word is his first novel.